The Space and Distance Between Us
cover painting by Claude Chapdelaine
Acrylic on canvas 30" x 48"

Gay Soulmate Wanted !

by

Charles Seems

Library and Archives Canada Cataloguing in Publication

Seems, Charles, author

Gay soulmate wanted! / Charles Seems.

Issued in print and electronic formats.

ISBN 978-1-927032-59-6 (paperback).
--ISBN 978-1-927032-61-9 (PDF).
--ISBN 978-1-927032-60-2 (ebook)

I. Title.

PS8637.E4453G39 2016   C813'.6   C2016-906617-7

C2016-906618-5

Bookman 10/12
Comic Sans MS 12, 16

Design and editing
Peter Geldart
Danielle Aubrey
Petra Books
petrabooks.ca

This book is dedicated to two friends, Ed Gargel (Naples, Florida) and Patrick Larabie (Gatineau, Québec) who passed away within weeks of each other. They have left an incredible void. Each in their own way has greatly contributed to society and will be remembered for their generosity, kindness and sense of humour.

I would like to acknowledge Marie Allard for providing useful comments and directions.

And finally, I want to thank my spouse Robert for believing in me and for nudging me along when the writing became tedious. Without his constant support, this book would not have been finished.

This is a work of fiction. Names, characters, businesses, places, events, positions held and incidents are either the products of the author's imagination or used in a fictitious manner. Any resemblance to actual persons, living or dead, or actual events is purely coincidental.

Seems

Also by Charles Seems

The Road to Dalhousie: Memories from the North Shore
(petrabooks.ca 2013)

Ready, Set, Hired : A Practical Guide to Starting a Career with
the Canadian Government/Préparation, Action, Embauche :
Un guide pratique pour amorcer une carrière au sein du
gouvernement canadien
(GSPH.com);

Drug-Free Arthritis : Secrets to Successful Living
(amazon.com)

Seems

Table of Contents

Seems

Seems

1

A Difficult Discussion

'You can't be serious! I don't believe you! You really went out with a 39 year old man? Since when have you been cruising at Shady Pines?' asked the tall blonde sitting at the next table in the Centretown Pub on Somerset Street. 'Can people that old still get it up?'

It was a full house that night at the Somerset Street watering hole as students were back in town for the start of another year at university. A festive mood prevailed. Laughter came from all corners of the joint. The stunning blonde man was unconcerned about who could hear them. They spoke freely and without reserve.

'You're such a drama queen,' shouted the more demure of the two young men sitting at a table so close to mine it was as if we were all together. 'You must think that everyone over 30 is ancient.'

'Aren't they?' the blonde bombshell interjected.

'Vicious!' replied his table mate.

'Really! You actually enjoyed being with that old geezer? I bet he paid you well,' came the quick reply.

'I might be a slut, but I'm no rent boy!' countered the brown-haired guy who at this point was sliding down in his chair so as not to be too obvious in case someone who knew him overheard this bitchy exchange.

'Damn good thing, cause you'd starve to death.'

Having just turned 39 a few days earlier, the sting of the conversation was enough for me to get up and leave, but instead I stayed seated in my chair pondering the meaning of those words that were not meant for me but had assuredly hit home. Of all the things I had faced when I came out of the closet, the fear of growing older, at twice the pace of straight society, was the single scariest eventuality I did not want to hear about. When you're a young gay man, you can date men your own age or older but when you get older, most guys your age only want fresh meat. At 39 years of age, I was definitely 78 in gay years; no longer was I the cutie. How does an old fart like me find the love of his life? Depression was beginning to set in.

I had been single for years. Having abandoned the idea of falling in love with a man, I had resigned myself to live the rest of my years as a spinster, a dirty old man as I used to call anyone over 40. In time, I had become what I loathed the most: an older man, who can't find anyone his own age who is half decent and available, and has to consider younger males at the expense of being labelled a 'dirty old fart'.

On a cold Wednesday evening in December 1991, I sat in the living room listening to the evening news as I did every day after a hearty meal. It felt comfortable being at home on a stormy night in Ottawa. My mind was racing from one thing to another. So much was going on in my life yet nothing really important was impacting my day-to-day living.

Another winter was upon us. A season I hated as a child — still do! It always amazed me that some people enjoyed the cold and the snow; somehow they manage to make the best of it. Not me! As far as I can remember, I took very little pleasure in playing in the snow. Although I skied when I was very young, I can't remember why I gave it up. I enjoyed outdoor skating but only if the wind was gentle so that my skin could handle the cold. Someone once told me that the word snow was an acronym that means *shit no one wants*! The longer I lived, the more I believed it.

A loud bang from the street below brought me back to reality: a rush-hour noise probably from a car accident nearby. It was almost 6:30 pm when I realized that I had to get moving. I had agreed to facilitate a gay men's discussion group at the Sandy Hill Community Centre. I would have to forego the peace and tranquility of my apartment and get myself into my car to drive a kilometer and a half. As the crow flies, it was a much shorter distance, but the Centre was on the east side of the Rideau Canal which meant I had to drive to the nearest bridge to get to Sandy Hill. With heavy snow coming down, traffic would be slower than usual so I left earlier than I would have normally.

My trusted Honda Civic would get me there and back without a hitch. I knew I would keep this vehicle for a very long time. Maintenance was minimal; the car was made solidly. It was by far the most dependable automobile I had owned. As expected, I reached the Sandy Hill address in plenty of time, and parked at the rear of the building which had direct access to the lower level where the men's discussion group was being held.

Once inside, I met with the organizers of the group to go over the logistics of the evening. Accustomed to leading large group discussions, I should not have been nervous at the prospect of presiding, as most of the attendees were people I knew well, perhaps too well. I was fearful that I would lose control of the group if the discussion became heated. As always, I fretted about things that I ought not to have been concerned about. Being the perfectionist that I have always been, I wanted a perfect outcome. In my books, smooth sailing was the only way to go.

A few guys had come early and were helping me set up the room by arranging the chairs in a large circle capable of accommodating approximately 35 to 40 people. None of these guys were my type. Too big. Too small. Not enough personality! There was always something missing, something not quite right. Was I being fussy? Hard to please? Way too picky for my own good? Average would not cut it for me. Although I hadn't joined the group to meet Mr. Right, every Wednesday night was another opportunity to meet new people. Fresh faces and new ideas were welcomed; it kept all of us on our toes.

The Sandy Hill Community Centre consisted of many rooms; most of them were occupied every weeknight. Invariably, people came to the large space on the lower level thinking that an AA meeting or some other group gathering was planned. They were politely shooed away although some of the men were so handsome that we wished that they had stayed. On any given night, half a dozen strays needed to be redirected. While setting up the room, several people came to the door and figured out that they were at the wrong place. They quickly left before somebody saw them at the entrance of a room where gay men were about to congregate. At times, I wondered if some of them were testing themselves to see if they had the guts to attend a gay discussion group. Could I have been the perfect Martha Stewart hostess and persuaded some of them to stay? For the most part, I did not care if they joined us or not; they were of no special interest to me. Every once in a while, there was an exceptional man who showed up. Tonight, one such specimen looked at me and turned around. My happy face had not yet been applied, I thought to myself. Oh well, more will come. There seemed to be an endless supply of hunks with nothing better to do on a Wednesday evening than to make my heart go a flutter.

Difficult as it was to choose a subject of interest to a diverse group of gay men, I had selected gay marriage as my main topic. I wanted to hear different opinions on the subject of making a commitment to another person either through marriage or some other form of civil union. I fully expected that some of the participants would think the whole idea completely stupid or absurd. I had often heard the comment that gays should not follow in the footsteps of heterosexual couples for fear of winding up in similar predicaments when the relationship ends. Many felt that the legal entanglements were not worth the benefits of marriage regardless of the form it took.

'The majority of people see gay men as perverts, and unstable individuals incapable of remaining faithful to another', came the unexpected comment from the floor.

'Yet, we have numerous examples of long-term relationships that have worked. Could we not focus on these to make our point? Just as in opposite-sex couples, the definition of monogamy is one that is arrived at through discussion,' a third person might say.

'And what about the legal issues, child adoption issues?' would certainly be asked by those that had given thought to this burgeoning concept.

Although this was not what I wanted, not what I had hoped for, nor what I expected, it was my belief that I would remain without a life partner for the remainder of my days. Was I being presumptuous in choosing the gay marriage theme? Gutsy perhaps. However, I had strong opinions and I was hoping to hear how others felt about this touchy subject. It didn't take long after introductions (people and theme) that the more vocal guys started to weigh in.

'I can't see why we want to be like straight people!' said the first participant.

'Why would we want the legal trappings of heterosexual couples? Isn't the fact that we are gay and different, thus allowing us more freedom with respect to relationships, be a good enough reason to reject the notion of the conformity required if we were allowed to be wedded?' added the next person.

The discussion then took a life of its own as the group talked about promiscuity that is rampant in the gay world. Sex in the bushes at Remic Rapids was a hot topic in the Ottawa gay community. Would respectable and solid relationships be a way of encouraging guys to commit to monogamous relationships? Would society have a greater respect for gay couples who have wed and therefore supposedly have renounced or reduced promiscuity? Would marriage force couples to work through the tough times in order to keep their relationships alive? It had always been so easy to find someone, and then dispose of that person at the first sign of trouble or after the first major disagreement. Would marriage have an impact on the way gay men look at relationships?

'I, for one, will never marry. I think the idea is preposterous!' said Mark.

'If straight people are divorcing at such high rates, why the hell would we want to be married? Isn't the freedom of being single and gay what we treasure the most?' added Gerry in an attempt to support Mark's assertion.

There was no consensus in the room and none was being sought. It was, however, very indicative of the degree of divergence on this delicate topic. I wondered if anyone in the room was going to ask why I wasn't in a relationship. The answer would have been simple. I had not found the right person and I had no desire to build a relationship with a less-than-ideal mate. Oh yes, I had had my fair share of short courtships ranging from a few weeks to a few years but none that would have made me want to commit fully. I had met and dated some wonderful guys: some good looking, some less so. Some were promising, and in a few cases I really fell deeply in love and felt so hurt when it was over. I had been pained so many times that the mere thought of it happening again sent me running in the opposite direction when I met someone who was a strong candidate.

Before the evening was over, there was discussion about having a Christmas party but no decision was made. At break time, some of the guys had mentioned that it would be nice to get together informally but there were no firm suggestions offered up. As usual, at end of the evening, those who still wanted to further socialize gathered at Rosa's, a Mexican diner up the street. I usually joined the gang as I got to know people much better in the smaller and more intimate setting of this restaurant.

2

Angels Before Me

By the middle of the following week, the cold weather abated and an increase in the thermometer caused the freshly-fallen snow to evaporate; roads were back to asphalt and sidewalks were dry. This was not unusual, as every year in Ottawa there is no guarantee that we will have a white Christmas. Despite my lack of enthusiasm about winter, a little snow on or before December 25th was more than welcomed.

1991 was coming to a close. It had been a remarkable 12 months. In December, the Ukrainian people voted for independence. On the last day of the month we saw the dissolution of the USSR. The collapse of the Soviet Union had been looming for some time; this was no surprise to anyone. It was, however, a significant milestone in the history of the world. I had never imagined that the day would come in my lifetime when one of the two largest superpowers would face such drastic changes. The painful history of Russia's tsarist, communist, and capitalist regimes had brought the Union to a point of no return.

My interest in world affairs was certainly due to my father's curiosity for political events happening in our country or elsewhere. An American by birth, he seldom missed the evening news. Although not much was happening in my life at that time, there was always plenty going on around the world.

My biggest preoccupation at the time was my brother's health. In August, my sister Claire had informed me that Geoff had been diagnosed with mycosis fungoides, a relatively rare disease where lymphocytes (a type of white blood cell) become malignant (cancerous) and affect the skin. His prognosis was not optimistic and doctors were baffled by the numerous side effects of the medication he was being administered. My brother's condition was on my mind day and night. Not much else mattered to me.

Remarkably, I was able to function well at work. I needed to stay involved in social activities to keep my spirits up. At the time, I was heavily involved in Lambda Ottawa, a network of gay professionals who met on a monthly basis. Our regular meetings took place in alternating restaurants. At each event, an invited speaker would talk about things that were happening in our city that affected the gay community. It was a not-to-be-missed social event; I met many great guys. I was encouraged to join the Executive of Lambda. Fearing that my lack of experience would not be appreciated, I nonetheless reluctantly agreed to stand for office and stayed for several years.

The francophone gay men's discussion group was another social outlet I enjoyed. The last meeting of the year was planned for December 11th. As I was not facilitating that night, I would be able to enjoy the evening without the added pressure of being in the spotlight.

The discussion group meeting attracted a huge crowd for this mid-December offering. Close to 40 people showed up; some came in after the discussion had started. The topic of the evening was 'What impact does being gay have on celebrating Christmas?' Contrary to themes where only a few people had strong opinions, most people wanted to speak their mind about how they dealt with Christmas. It was an animated discussion with few contrary positions. Most felt that it was a difficult time of the year for them particularly those that were single and the ones that had been rejected by their family for being who they were.

My mind left the conversation as I wasn't that interested in the topic. I looked around the room to see who was there. Two guys sitting across the circle from me were smiling at each other. Mark Lafontaine had often come to the discussion group meetings but was always unaccompanied. I knew he lived alone and that he wasn't involved with anyone at the time. Could this be a budding romance? I knew Mark as he came regularly to Lambda Ottawa dinner meetings.

Two others came in late. Henry Moran and someone I had never seen before. They had made quite an entrance not by being boisterous but rather by their colorful clothing. The visitor wore a bright red jacket which was hard to miss. He was impeccably dressed in dark dress pants, white shirt with black pin stripes and a red v-neck sweater. His infectious smile caught my eye.

'Let's take a fifteen minute break!' said the evening's facilitator.

I sprang to my feet as I saw Henry and the stranger walking across the floor in my direction.

'Rick, I would like you to meet an old buddy of mine,' Henry said with a broad smile.

'Pleasure meeting you,' I said looking at this hunk of a man close up. 'I don't recall ever seeing you here before,' I added.

'In fact, you have,' he responded immediately. 'I was here last week, but I don't think you saw me,' he hastened to add.

'Sorry, but I can't remember. I was a little stressed last week and much of that evening is a blur,' I explained.

'Help yourself to juice and cookies,' I said to the newbie as I walked away in the direction of the table where the refreshments were located.

I overheard a conversation about having a Christmas party for the group. Again this week, not a single person was coming up with concrete ideas or plans. I thought it would be a good idea to invite the guys to my apartment on O'Connor Street on Friday night. As many of them would be going out to the bars and one of the most popular places at the time (CP) was just around the corner from where I lived, I figured many would come and leave early to go bar hopping. After the break, I made the invitation.

'I have decided to invite you all to a house party at 250 O'Connor, suite 11 on Friday, December 13th at 8 pm' I said, to the amazement of many in the room.

I could tell that my announcement had been well received and the group organizers seemed relieved that some form of Christmas event would be happening. To make sure that everyone felt welcomed, I would need to speak to a few people in the room before the night was over. Would I be able to entice this new arrival in coming? Perhaps he'd come if Henry came with him.

Henry and his friend stood together chatting for the duration of the break. I glanced over a few times trying not to be too obvious. Perhaps I would be able to entice Henry to join the regulars who were going to a restaurant after the meeting. The mystery man seemed shy and somewhat reserved. Did he come from a big or small family? He seemed somewhat intimidated by the crowd. Maybe he had just come out of the closet and wasn't comfortable around so many gay men. Would he feel comfortable enough to join us in a public place? Could he be convinced to come to the Christmas party?

At approximately 8:30 the meeting was over; the facilitator mentioned that some guys in the group would be going for coffee at Rosa's. I gathered my things and went to speak to a few newcomers to make sure they felt included in the invitation for Friday night. I kept glancing back to see if the new guy was still in the room. He and Henry were chatting, obviously in no rush to leave. I walked over to them and asked whether or not they intended to join us for coffee. To my surprise, the answer was yes. Henry never joined us at Rosa's Cantina; this was a first. That night, he had an air about him; he was proud as a peacock. Would we find out that this beautiful man was Henry's new partner?

We left our vehicles in the Community Centre parking lot and walked up Somerset Street East as far as King Edward Avenue where the restaurant was located. We sat in groups of four. At my table were Henry, his friend and Gordon, who at first appeared mildly interested in Henry's partner but whose interest grew exponentially as the evening wore on. He was very obviously smitten by this intriguing person. I too was keen on getting to know this new kid on the block; I asked a number of personal questions which he answered with ease. The more I found out about him, the more I thought he was a well-balanced individual capable of expressing himself rather well. What I found out was that he came from a small family; he had no brothers and only one sister. His father was in business and managed a number of companies for which he provided administrative support. It was obvious that this was a close-knit family and the relationship between father and son was very strong.

All of this was music to Gordon's ears as he was in a very similar situation. He connected with him on many levels and they shared stories about the business world. Gordon's father had been in business for years and wanted his son to take over when he retired. Gordon wasn't sure that he wanted to follow in his father's footsteps, at least not without a partner. This young man, new to us all, would be an ideal associate and potentially a spouse. It was obvious that Gordon was falling for him and that he was hoping to leave Rosa's Cantina with him. That was not to be; we all left at the same time and walked back to the parking lot. Henry and his guest drove off leaving Gordon a tad perplexed. Before they got into their cars, I reminded them of the party.

Barely 48 hours later, I'd be hosting a party for an unspecified number of gay men. Estimating that about 20 people would show up, I immediately started to prepare. Had I been too hasty in deciding to have this party in my apartment? Would this be a foolish decision I would live to regret? It was too late to turn back now and furthermore, the thought of seeing this gorgeous man in my apartment washed away any fears I was harboring at the time. *Thou shall not covet your best friend's new partner,* I thought to myself. He was younger, good looking, taller, and obviously much sought after. I hadn't been looking to get into a relationship and was in no hurry to get involved lest I get hurt as I had been the previous year. Would I get myself in trouble with Henry? Perhaps they weren't an item! Did I stand a chance? If this was meant to happen, it would; if not, there would be other fish in the sea. But for now, he was an angel and nothing could take away from the wonderful feeling I had when I thought of him. If not him, perhaps Don might show up and sweep me off my feet. Donald Goldberg, a well-placed public servant, was intelligent, engaging and a terrific chef. There was always a twinkle in his right eye when he spoke to me. He had the right stuff. Just a tad older than I, his life experiences had been varied; he had learned a lot over the years and would make a perfect husband. He too would be at the party, another good-looking man to spice up the ho-hum group that we were.

3

Friday the 13th

Luck would have it that the Christmas party fell on a Friday the 13th. Had I been superstitious, I might not have agreed to that date. I could have easily invited the crowd for the following evening on December 14th, but experience had demonstrated that it was always easier to get people to come to a party on a Friday night especially on short notice. Plans for Saturdays were normally set well ahead of time therefore fewer people would have been able to show up had I tried to avoid the ominous date. Delaying a week would have brought it too close to the Holidays when many leave Ottawa to go back home for Christmas.

On my way back from work, I started to think about what needed to be done in order to be ready for the party. Cleaning the apartment would be top priority. My downtown apartment right in the heart of what would eventually become the 'gay village' was without a doubt my pride and joy. The three-story red brick walk-up built in the 1930s exuded charm that newer buildings could never match. It had been a stroke of luck to find this place after I had already rented a much less appealing apartment several streets over. My friend Michael had to convince me that the difference in rent would be offset by the number of years I would stay put in that building, as I would not likely want to move out to find better accommodations.

Connor Court, as it was called, had been renovated; Suite 11 was being used as the model apartment. Beautiful leaded windows in every room including the washroom faced either south onto McLaren Street or east onto O'Connor Street. With beautiful refinished hard-wood floors and high ceilings, this 1200 square foot unit had a generous living room and dining room but a tiny galley kitchen. As you entered, a small square vestibule led into a rectangular hallway with arches leading into the dining room to the right and straight ahead into the living room. An art deco plaster fireplace and mantel was the focus of the living room, and each year at Christmas, it was decorated with red candles.

Furnished with a mix of modern furniture and antiques, I had wanted my home to be stylish and without ostentation. Both form and function had been considered in the purchase of each item. I had chosen not to put up curtains as to not take away the view from the leaded windows. Where privacy was needed, I had purchased recycled church-styled stained glass windows that were hung between the outer windows and the window casings. The beige, black, grey, navy and rust color scheme used throughout the apartment worked well with the eclectic mix of furnishings I had accumulated over the years.

Born under the sign of Virgo, perfection is the goal in all things. Not only did I concern myself with my surroundings, I was also focused on what I would be wearing for the party. Had it not been for the possibility that two or three interesting men would attend, I would not have spent quite as much time trying to figure out what outfit I would don. I liked the 'sophisticated but relaxed' look that had sprung up in the interior design as well as in the fashion industry. Comfortable and chic would be my guiding principles for what I would wear. In the end, I chose a pair of blue jeans, a black silk shirt with a candy red silk bowtie.

Shortly before 8 pm, the first guests started to arrive. The crowd grew quickly. Don arrived alone which indicated that he was still available, or so I thought. At about 8:45, Henry and his friend arrived carrying their refreshments for the evening. A B.Y.O.B. (bring you own booze) was standard practice in those days allowing each person to decide on what and how much they wanted to consume. I kidded Henry about the fact that he had not told me his buddy's name. 'Sorry, Joshua is the name,' he said, sheepishly knowing that he had been remiss in not properly introducing us earlier. I shook hands with Joshua repeating his name as I gazed into his eyes. Henry and Joshua then made their way to the kitchen to put beer in the refrigerator. Meanwhile, I went around chatting with everyone making sure that each person felt welcomed. Returning to the kitchen for more munchies, I noticed that Joshua had not moved an inch. Fearing that he felt left out, I made several trips to the kitchen and spoke to him each time.

As expected, around 10:30 pm the first to leave wanted to go dancing at CP. Gradually the crowd shrunk leaving just a handful of people who lingered till midnight. Unexpectedly, Henry announced that he was leaving. I assumed that Joshua would he heading out with him, however, I was wrong. The party had shifted to the kitchen where at least four people all standing shoulder-to-shoulder were having a great time. Joshua seemed to be the centre of attention. His huge smile and white teeth couldn't be missed. He roared every time a funny line or story was told. Standing next to Joshua, I boldly put one arm on his left shoulder. Without realizing it, I must have given those around us the signal to leave; all were gone shortly after.

'I'll help you clean-up,' Joshua said as the last person left the party.

'That would be really appreciated,' I said, seeing the amount of work that needed to be done.

'Just tell me where you store your cleaning products and I'll get rolling,' he added.

In less than an hour, we had finished the job. Expecting Joshua to want to leave as it was by now very late, I wondered if I could entice him to stay a bit longer. I was dying to find out whether or not he was attached to Henry.

'Oh, we're just good friends' he replied. 'For years, we have been sharing information about our respective music collections.'

Relieved that he wasn't Henry's new recruit, I asked him to sit down with me and have a drink. As we watched the snow fall very softly to the ground to the sounds of easy listening music played on CIMF, the mood was enhanced by all the Christmas decorations. A string of bright red candles burning on the mantel helped to create the perfect romantic atmosphere for getting to know each other. Cuddled in the corner of the L-shaped sofa, Joshua and I took turns asking each other questions about family, goals, career, expectations, etc. In law, this would be called 'discovery' and it sure was in our case as we disclosed to each other information that would ordinarily be shared much later in a relationship.

'Do your parents know you are gay?' I asked.

'Oh yes,' was his reply. 'My Mother has no problems dealing with it, but I think my Dad would prefer that I not speak about it. It seems to make him uncomfortable whenever the topic of homosexuality is brought up. I guess it's a generational thing and I can't expect him to understand. As long as he tolerates me, I'm okay with him not being pleased that he has a gay son.'

So many things crossed my mind in the time it took to ask the next question. Did he mind that his father did not or could not embrace the fact that he was gay? Did the situation create tensions at home? Would my presence exacerbate things at home for him?

'Did you come here tonight with the intention of knowing more about me?' I ventured to ask.

'Oh, I know a lot about you already. I've done my research,' he said looking at me straight in the eyes to see my reaction. Without the benefit of a mirror, I could not see my expressions, but I'm almost sure that his words did have an impact on me and that my face certainly told him a lot about what I was feeling.

'That's unfair, I know so little about you,' I said.

'I have nothing to hide,' he said, 'just ask and I'll answer any and all questions you might have.'

'OK you're on,' I said excitedly. 'What do you value the most in a relationship?'

The answer to that question revealed that he valued honesty, loyalty and kindness the most. Friendships were not to be taken lightly; he had been extremely close to his grandfathers in whom he confided on a regular basis. With the recent passing of his paternal grandfather with whom he had a very special bond, he felt that he needed to establish new relationships albeit very different than those he had experienced with his grandparents.

It was quite obvious to me that Joshua was looking for a soulmate. His questions had been probing as if to confirm what he was thinking or perhaps what he had heard about me. Many people in the community knew me well so getting information about my interests, my values and my goals would not have been difficult to do.

Sitting next to him on the sofa and watching him tell me his life story, I began to look at him closely. At 6 feet, he was a few inches taller than me. There was no fat on his lean frame although he wasn't muscular. His thick brown hair and brown eyes with incredibly long eyelashes gave him an air of sophistication. Traces of severe acne cleared up long ago did not diminish his facial good looks. A prominent nose was the marking of a solid man, I thought to myself. There were no feminine mannerisms and no affectations of any sort. He was genuine, an original boy next door kind of guy. The more I observed, the more I liked what I was seeing.

Joshua admitted that he had been attracted to me for some time. In fact, he mentioned to someone that he was my boyfriend but was bluntly told that this could not be true as everyone knew that Richard Steeves was dating a handsome man from Montréal. Little did he know about the Steeves family from Dalhousie, New Brunswick, a middle class family into which were born six children all with blue eyes like their father. As a middle child, I felt different. There was enough love to go around but somehow I saw myself as an outcast, a square peg in a round hole. I had no interest in sports, had no physical strength or any desire to acquire any and was not competitive in the least. The word 'sissy' comes to mind and in fact it had been used in reference to me many times in my early days in Dalhousie. Growing up in a red-neck town and not fitting into the crowd makes one want to leave as soon as possible which is what I did at the age of 14. Going to a private school 50 miles away was like running away from reality, but certainly the best decision I made as a teenager in the throes of becoming a young gay man with way too many urges and desires. Joshua knew nothing about my past; it would take some time before I would unravel a story that would surprise him more than I expected.

'You probably don't remember,' said Josh, 'but on October 30th, I was introduced to you by my friend Mark in the lobby of the Archives building on Wellington Street just before the 'Wilde about Sappho' public readings.'

'Really?' I said. 'Sorry, but I'm don't recall much about that evening. I was preoccupied with my brother's health.'

'We sat a few rows in front of you, while you sat alone behind us,' he continued. 'I really wanted to go sit with you, but I felt that you wanted to be alone.'

'Now that I think about it,' I said, 'I thought you were Mark's partner and I didn't pay much attention to you for fear of showing interest. Just now, I'm realizing that you are friends with two people I know: Mark and Henry. That explains why I saw you talking to Mark the evening you came to the gay men's discussion group. What a small world!'

'That's not the only time I saw you,' he added. 'You were at the Nepean Centrepointe Theatre for a late summer performance by the Ottawa Men's Chorus, were you not?' he asked.

'Yes, I was,' I said. 'Gerald was in from Montréal and we had decided to attend the OMC Pride Week concert.'

'I wasn't stalking you,' he quickly added, 'I figured out where I was likely to see you.'

'You've must have known that I often went to the gay men's discussion group meetings on Wednesdays,' I enquired.

'Henry had told me that if I wanted to meet you, that would probably be the best place,' he proffered.

'So that's why you came on December 11th?' I said as I winked at him.

'Actually, I first went to the discussion group meeting on the 4th of December but I don't think you noticed me,' Joshua said. 'I arrived early so that I would be able to speak to you privately in the lobby. I wanted to avoid having to go into the meeting room. As most guys entered the building through the back door, the one closest to the parking lot, I knew that I would be able to see you as you came in, however, as it turned out, you had already arrived and your attention was focused on the men who wanted to get your advice about one thing or another. I don't think you were aware of my presence. Feeling very let down, I decided that there was no point in staying for the meeting. I drove back home in a nasty snow storm. I had come a long way to see you, but it didn't work out,' he added.

My heart fell to my heels as I realized that this person was really serious about me and that I hadn't even clued in to the fact that he was making every effort to meet me. Geoff's health issues had definitely taken a toll on my life and had it not been for Josh's determination, we would probably never have met.

4

A Long Night

There I sat with Joshua answering all of his questions on my past: not the Spanish Inquisition it could have become but rather a friendly dialogue with someone genuinely interested in me. Was I dreaming or was this really happening? It was getting late, much later than my normal bed time yet I had no desire to stop the conversation and get some sleep. This kind of opportunity came rarely and I wasn't going to abort what felt like the beginning of something great, or at least that's what I thought.

'How old are you?' I asked.

'I turned 29 in June,' Joshua replied.

'That makes me 10 years older than you,' I answered sheepishly. 'Will that be a problem for you? Could that be a problem for your family?'

'Can't see why!' said Josh.

'I'm turning 40 in September and I want to go to Europe to celebrate. I've never been there so this is a perfect excuse for the trip. I've been planning this for quite a while; nothing will stop me from going. If you want to come along, that would be great,' I said.

'How do you plan to travel around Europe?' Joshua enquired. 'Which countries will you visit? I might be interested in joining you; after all, I will be celebrating my 30th birthday on the third of June.'

By this time, I was getting the distinct impression that he was indeed very serious about pursuing a relationship. However, this trip would be nine months later; much could change during that period of time. It was too soon to know what the impediments might be but, in time, I would certainly discover the forces that might tear us apart.

Still intrigued that such a young, charming and attractive guy would be interested in me, I started probing Joshua to discover his basic values. Was his interest in me just a passing fancy or was he interested in a permanent, long term and committed relationship? Did he realize that I would be retiring 10 years before him? Had he thought that he might have to take care of an aging man?

'Wouldn't our ten-year age difference make it difficult for you as it will be obvious to friends and family?' I enquired.

'I think it will bother you more than me,' he snapped back. 'What difference can it make? And furthermore, the older we get, the less obvious that difference will be.'

'You're thinking long-term,' I gleefully stated then paused and waited for a reaction, which took no time to arrive.

'Long before we actually met, I had decided that you were the right person for me. For whatever reasons, I felt a strong connection to you and I still do. Don't get me wrong, it won't always be easy, but I'm willing to give it my best shot. The age difference is not an issue nor will it ever be. It's not because you're older that you will die first. Or get sick first. Either one of us could be pushing the wheelchair. I suggest you get over your worries and allow life to unfold as it should.'

For a 29-year-old who had yet to leave home, to leave the security of caring parents, he displayed a level of maturity that I could have never imagined for someone his age. A true Gemini, one minute he could be very serious and thoughtful and the next, Joshua could be howling with laughter at the least insignificant thing that struck him as funny.

Certainly Joshua could spark up my life. Being around him would give me a sense of purpose. His sense of humor would go a long way in making our nest egg a happy one as I found his brand of zaniness rather funny. I would need to make sure that he was the right person. Rather than jump in too quickly as I had done so many times in the past, restraint would be paramount. It wasn't like me to hold back. This would be hard!

'So Josh, what do value most in another person?' I asked.

'Honesty,' he answered without having to think about it. 'Trust and good judgment would be a close second.' We were covering ground that we had visited before but this time, it was getting a lot more personal. Instead of talking about relationship values, we were discussing personal values, beliefs and expectations without really calling them by name.

'How important is religion to you?' I asked.

He paused for a few minutes before I got an answer.

'If you're asking if I attend church, the answer is no,' said Joshua unequivocally. 'Long ago, I visited Rome and when I came back to Canada, I told my parents that I could no longer accept the teachings of a church that is always asking for money when, in fact, it owns the richest and most expensive art in the world.'

'I share your opinions on the Catholic Church,' I said, 'but for different reasons. As far as I am concerned, man-made religions are bound to be as weak as the men themselves that created them. The Catholic Church's position on homosexuality is arcane and counter to the concept of a loving God in whose image we were made. I believe in a supreme being regardless of the term used to describe him or her. Faith, hope and charity are at the root of my being and spiritualism is my guide.'

A warm hug from Joshua convinced me that we shared the same basic feeling about life, love and faith. He asked me about what I thought were the ingredients necessary for a relationship to work. My response was a rather long-winded discussion about what I considered to be the base of a strong relationship.

'Josh, from my perspective and experience, there are four important elements that either make or break a relationship.' I read aloud from a recent book: 'For two people to get along and love each other over a long period of time, there must be a healthy connection on the physical, intellectual, emotional, and spiritual aspects of life'. To make it perfectly clear to him, I added, 'I may be physically attracted to you but, if, on the intellectual level, we don't meet, there is not much hope that things will work out. Even if we felt we met each other on three of the four elements, lack of complementarity on a single element is enough to undermine the foundation of a healthy union.'

'Would you walk away from someone you felt strongly about because you knew the lack of similarity would eventually bring the relationship down?', he asked.

'Although the issue is not similarity but rather comple-mentarity, yes I would find a way to bow out without allowing myself to get too involved for fear of being hurt down the road,'

I said. 'I have not always chosen that path, sometimes preferring to go along for the ride knowing only too well that there was very little hope for a long term relationship.'

I realized that it was about 4 am and we still had much to share. Should I suggest we get to bed and talk more tomorrow? By this time, I figured he would be spending the night. Or what remained of it. Gambling that he would agree to a sleepover, I asked him if he wanted to stay. He smiled at me as if to say 'I thought you'd never ask'. I did not have a reputation of being easy and I suspected he had heard that I would not be hopping into bed with him at the first occasion. Yet there was no denying that I wasn't about to pass up the best prospect I had met in years.

'On what basis did you choose to come to Ottawa,' Joshua said while yawning away. 'Had you chosen any other place, we may not have met. Of all the cities in Canada, the nation's capital was not the most exciting place to be in the seventies. I'd be curious to know what made you decide on moving to Ottawa.'

'That's a long story Josh,' I said. 'It will have to wait till tomorrow.'

5

Choosing Ottawa

From a family where French and English were spoken on a daily basis, I could not imagine living in a place where only one language, one culture was present. I needed and wanted to maintain my linguistic abilities in Canada's two official languages.

Ruling out living in small towns due to the narrow mindedness of its citizenry, I opted for cities where self-expression would be encouraged. Being a gay man in the early seventies meant that, to live freely, one had to choose locales where being a homosexual would not get you into trouble.

I considered living in Moncton as I felt comfortable in this city of nearly 75,000 inhabitants. Although predominantly English speaking, the bedroom communities of Dieppe, Schédiac, Cap Pelé, etcetera ensured an endless supply of Acadians, and thus the French culture I needed to have in order to be happy. The only problem was that I had few friends there and the ones I had were moving to larger cities at the end of their studies. Some were moving to Québec City, others to Halifax, Montréal, Sherbrooke, Fredericton and even Hamilton.

Each of these places offered interesting possibilities but they were dismissed as being too big, too far, too French, too homophobic or too English for my taste. As I did not have a job lined up, I needed to consider the employment opportunities that would be available to me in a new city. Graduating with a degree in translation, a government town was an obvious choice. But my interest in working as a translator or interpreter had waned since the start of my studies in Moncton in 1976. I was no longer sure that I had made the best career choice. My bet was that, if I chose the right place to live, I could probably free-lance and earn some easy money while trying to find what type of career would suit me best. I narrowed the choices to Fredericton and Ottawa.

During my penultimate year of studies in Moncton, I had visited friends in Ottawa. One of them, Gerry, was a former university classmate now working for the Canada Mortgage and Housing Corporation. Doing well and living on Laurier Street in the heart of Ottawa, I was envious of his success. Gerry went to considerable expense and time to show me the best of what Ottawa had to offer. He had me convinced that choosing Ottawa would be a wise choice, one that I would never regret.

During the same weekend, I spent time with my hometown friend, Norman, who, with his partner Marc, lived in Old Chelsea. Although I preferred being downtown, I enjoyed the calm and serenity of this quaint village just a stone's throw from the metropolitan area. Norman and Marc were keen on having me share their apartment, if and when I chose to move to the Ottawa area. Norman had tried to further entice me by saying that he would help me find temporary employment. He and Marc worked at Café Luigi and would put in a good word on my behalf. With a bit of luck, I would be hired on.

In my final year at l'Université de Moncton, I shared an apartment with my good friend Frenchy. To her credit, she had already secured a position with the Canadian Government and all of her removal expenses to Ottawa would be paid by the Crown. Fredericton had lost its appeal as I did not have one close friend who was already living there. Furthermore, I had already lived there and found the city to be a bit small. Getting in and out by air was not the greatest. In that regard, Moncton was far more central and had better air links to major Canadian and American cities.

Over the years, I had not accumulated very much so that at the end of my studies in Moncton, my belongings could easily fit into 4-5 boxes. In addition to my clothes, I had acquired a small collection of books and records typical of what most students amassed over a period of four years of post-secondary education. I did not own a single piece of furniture although the desire to have some was beginning to form. Having so little to my name, moving my personal effects to another city would not be a problem.

It was Frenchy's idea that I should pack my stuff and label the boxes in a way that identified them as mine. She would add them to her stack of boxes for removal to Ottawa. That way, I could fly to Ottawa and not concern myself with my earthly treasures. They would eventually be delivered to an address on Friel Street from where I would retrieve them.

Neither Frenchy nor I felt any guilt in doing this. She had found out that a flat rate would be applied and that whether there were six boxes or sixteen, the cost was the same. Ironically, we had obtained the apartment which we shared on the assumption that we were a working-class couple and not students, so moving our belongings together was simply continuing the same white lie.

6

A Stormy Saturday

Breakfast in bed, I thought to myself; Joshua would certainly appreciate it. In a matter of minutes after getting up, I was back into the bedroom with toast and jam, a bowl of fruit and a glass of orange juice neatly placed on a tray.

'Your lordship is served,' I said.

'You didn't need to do this,' said Josh. 'This is the first time I ever had breakfast in bed.'

'Enjoy it!' I said. 'You may not get this kind of treatment often.'

'But what about the crumbs in bed?' he added.

'Not to worry, I'll take care of those,' I said. 'I don't often get the chance to spoil someone, so take it while it comes.'

By late morning, it had snowed considerably with no signs of letting up. The streets were getting clogged as the proverbial matter accumulated at a rapid pace. It seemed that the city was coming to a crawl on a normally busy Saturday morning. Ordinarily, I would have been running errands at this time, but I planned otherwise. Grocery shopping had been done on Thursday evening to avoid having to do it on Saturday, just in case a wonderful guy had decided to linger in my home.

We continued to explore each other's worlds by probing further. It had already been confirmed that we shared similar values, and were looking for a long-term and stable relationship based on trust and respect. Although we had different backgrounds, our family values were not that dissimilar. While he had been brought up in an upper-middle-class family, his family's wealth had not affected him negatively, or so it appeared. He didn't seem spoilt. Judging from the examples he provided of situations where his parents expected him to share in the development of the family businesses, I could tell that he had certainly worked hard to help secure their business success. It was obvious that he came from a close-knit family where hard work was expected but was also rewarded from time to time.

'Any plans for Christmas?' I asked.

'Yes,' Joshua answered. 'We own a condo in Florida and we will be spending a few weeks there. We will be leaving in a week... You look sad! Are you worried?'

'We won't be able to see each other for a while. You might forget me,' I said lamentingly.

'That won't happen,' Joshua assured me. 'I'll write you a postcard every day, I promise. It would help if I could get a recent picture of you that would help me remember what you look like.'

'You've got it,' I said. 'Just make sure that you don't leave it lying around. You wouldn't want to raise suspicions.'

It became clear to me that while Joshua still lived at home and that his parents knew he was gay, there wasn't a full acceptance of his homosexuality. He had had a few relationships but none that had lasted a long time. In all cases, his boyfriends had been in the same age bracket. Our ten-year difference would eventually cause concern but I was in no hurry to bring this to the fore. Although people told me that I look younger than my age, the same could be said of Josh. It was apparent that we weren't of the same cohort.

My fear, albeit a tad premature, was that Joshua might meet someone his own age and feel that he was missing out on life. Did he have any further wild oats to sow? Would he want to roam? I wondered if people would think that I was robbing the cradle. But that sentiment too was a bit over the top. He was about to turn 30; although he was still living with his parents, he was not an immature young man looking for a sugar daddy. I did worry that if we decided to live together, it would be awkward if not difficult for him to move out from the family homestead (a 4000 square foot sprawling home on four levels) into a very modest two-bedroom apartment. My world would be changing substantially with his arrival at Connor Court, but his move would be drastic. It had always been my opinion that everyone should experience living alone at least once in their life and that the best time to do this is when one is young. It's a wonderful learning experience that Joshua would miss if he moved in with me straight from home.

Nevertheless, I would not encourage him to do so for fear of losing him altogether. I was getting way ahead of myself; I couldn't help seeing the many twists and turns our relationship would take. True to myself and with a *Qué sera, sera* mentality, I moved away from those dark thoughts.

'Getting a tad hungry?' I asked.

'Yes,' Joshua replied. 'Should we go out for a bite to eat?'

'Take a look out the window,' I said. 'What would you say if we stayed home? I'll heat up some soup and make sandwiches.'

'Sounds good to me,' said Josh.

Into the galley kitchen I went to get us some food to last us for the afternoon. Joshua stayed in the living room admiring the artwork and perusing my music collection. Every once in a while, he would see something for which he wanted more information. He'd come to the kitchen entrance to ask about what he had seen and when he got his answer, he would go back to the living room to continue his discovery. Through a person's possessions, one can pick up a lot of information and this was exactly what he was doing. I felt comfortable that he wanted to know more about me. If he felt at home in my apartment, then it would make it easier on us later on.

We sat at a small gate-leg table in front of the dining room window. The room was big enough to have a large circular glass-top table for six and a small, more intimate breakfast table. We ate slowly as we continued to talk about the upcoming Christmas holidays. For once in a long while, it felt like Christmas as the snow continued to fall very lightly, blanketing the trees and the red brick homes and apartment dwellings on MacLaren and O'Connor Streets. From our window on the second level, it felt like we were looking at a Cornelius Krieghoff painting. Despite my dislike of the colder months, I had a fondness for winter scenes. I attributed this to my early childhood in northern New Brunswick where snow would start in early November and stay until the end of April. I hated the long winters, but the whiteness and purity of snow frosting everything in sight making every scene appear as though out of a fairy tale had long been imprinted in my memory. Those days when schools had to close, when the snow plows remained in the town garage as the weather was so bad, we got a day off school to play. It was pure joy not only to avoid classes but to frolic in the mounds of white snow that filled our back yard. It was a safe environment, one in which every parent was happy to allow their child to go outdoors. In those early years, snow was still impressive, I hadn't yet learned to dislike it.

'You seem far away,' said Josh.

'I was just reminiscing about my childhood in Dalhousie,' I said. 'I was recalling the fun I had with my friends building forts and caves in the back yard. Caves were especially enjoyable as they were private domains in which one felt a sense of privacy and ownership. We used candles to light the interiors. The soft light provided an atmosphere of peace and tranquility. At times, it felt romantic; however, dressed in layers of clothes, nothing untoward ever happened in those sub-zero dwellings, although I often suspected that my Mother thought that my friend and I were doing nasty things.'

'Let's clean up and go for a walk in the snow,' suggested Josh.

Dressed warmly, we walked along Somerset in the direction of Elgin Street, all the while admiring the trees laden with snow, their branches bent as far as they could go under the weight of the heavy white accumulation of the past 12 hours. Shoppers were rushing home with their treasures. All along the street, we heard the sounds of Christmas music playing softly. Wreaths and bells hung in storefronts adding to the charm of this lovely area of town. The village atmosphere of Elgin Street between Lisgar and McLeod was at its highest peak of the year. In the Golden Triangle, as it is affectionately called, you could sense the feeling of belonging as people passed each other smiling and wishing one another Merry Christmas. We walked as far as Gladstone heading west towards Bank Street. Although not as intimate as Elgin Street, there was a lot happening on this busy thoroughfare with people going in and out of shops. On our final stretch, we walked along Somerset between Bank and O'Connor Street so that we could admire big Victorian mansions housing restaurants, bars, and offices. One of the buildings was new; the old structure had burnt to the ground and City Hall had forced the developer to rebuild in the original architectural style. A unique historical block of houses did not fail to impress Joshua.

It was plain to see that we enjoyed each other's company. Back at the apartment, we continued to talk about how the Christmas holidays would unfold and anticipated the hardship of being apart. I sensed that Joshua would have wanted us to see each other again before he and his family left for Florida but that would prove to be almost impossible. Knowing that his parents would likely wonder where he was as he had not called since leaving the house the night before, I suggested that he should let his Mother know that he was safe in Ottawa.

After he hung up, Joshua explained that his parents were indeed worried about his whereabouts as the weather was expected to get worse on Saturday evening. With sadness in our eyes, we hugged each other before Joshua left for Gatineau. I wondered if I would ever see him again. I wondered if he would remember me. Would he meet a more interesting person in Florida and drop me like a hotcake? I took comfort in the fact that we had spent 36 wonderful hours together. *Qué sera, sera*, I said to myself as I started thinking about what I would make for dinner.

Plans got changed: I learned from Joshua that the trip to Florida had been cancelled when he called on the following Wednesday night. There was no stated reason for the cancellation; secretly I was thrilled as this meant Joshua and I would be spending time together during the holidays although I knew I would not see him on Christmas day. It would have been inappropriate to show excitement about the abrupt change of plans; I empathized with Joshua about the missed opportunity to spend Christmas in the Deep South.

My exhilaration was short lived. Two days later, Joshua called to say that they would indeed be leaving for Florida on December 21st.

7

A Lonely Christmas

Anticipating that the Christmas season would be more painful than usual, I made sure that I had a number of outings planned. My friend Mary who had recently separated from her husband made plans that included me. On Christmas Eve, along with her son and daughter, we attended the children's mass. I arrived at their townhouse in Centrepointe dressed to the nines. As I entered the house, Susie was in the stairwell checking me out. *Don we now our GAY apparel, fa-la-la, la-la-la, la la la* I sang out to her loud cheers of approval.

Not having young children to share the joy of Christmas does not make for happy times. Mary's children compensated enormously and their exuberance for all things festive helped to fill the void in my life. The smiles on their faces as they witnessed the skaters perform flawlessly at the Ice Capades show were priceless. They weren't my children but they could have been as I cared deeply for them. Intelligent and witty, Susie and Mike were typical teenagers trying their best to get what they wanted out of Mom. Mary's encouragement and patience towards them made me feel that the warm family atmosphere that existed in their home was very real. I enjoyed being in their presence particularly when I missed my own siblings.

After my Mother's passing in 1984, Christmas day was meaningless. The family no longer got together at that time of the year as it was difficult to get everyone to travel to Northern New Brunswick when the weather was usually so foul. Although my Dad was alive, it was my Mother who made Christmas such a magical time. I longed to turn back the clock so that I could once again enjoy all the Christmas family traditions. Try as I might, nothing and nobody could help me with my feelings of desolation.

One person who could sense my sadness was Gerry. I could always count on him to invite me for Easter, Thanksgiving and Christmas dinners. He and his deaf mute spouse, Richard, were the quintessential hosts. Together, they made exquisite meals complete with decorations to suit the holiday. A pie maker extraordinaire, Gerry seldom missed an opportunity to bake a fruit pie that would rival any of those made by our mothers.

When invited to Gerry and Richard's for dinner, one would never know ahead of time who would be there. This couple knew many people in the gay community and rounded up all of those who were alone so that nobody would be spending time without friends during the holidays. Their generosity knew no bounds; often times, we would be eight to ten sitting around a crowded table. Wine flowed, joints were passed around to increase appetite and to relax the anal types, such as myself. Humor was Gerry's trademark; he tried very hard to make others laugh and enjoy themselves, even though he himself was going through some difficult health issues that he avoided talking about for fear of bringing down the party. Whether it was at their annual Oscar's party or Halloween, you were sure to have the time of your life.

Naturally, once the parties were over and reality set in, I would feel miserable again. Shopping, even without purchasing anything, was enough to revive my spirits. I would do this with regularity especially during the warmer months. Going in and out of stores with a heavy jacket in the colder periods of the year was not my idea of fun. Back in the 1970's, the Ottawa crowd went to Montréal to shop as there was much more variety and at prices we could not find in Ottawa; but driving to Montréal was risky; the road conditions were often rough and it got dark so early in the day.

Few people had been told about Josh; I kept that information veiled not wanting to sound too boastful in case it all fell apart. One of the people I had opened up to was Mary, my pragmatic friend knowing that I would hear her frank point of view. *Life is full of surprises*, I thought to myself; who really knows for sure what will come of this.

The year 1992 began with a turkey dinner at Mary's home with her kids on January 1. Although I hadn't said anything to her about Joshua not writing to me, I could have sworn she was reading my heart.

To cheer me up, Mary had planned a murder mystery evening. Great, I thought to myself. The promised postcards failed to materialize leaving me to wonder whether I had been foolish to think this young man cared at all. By the following week, Joshua and his family would be back in Canada and I'll know then where I stand. Time would go by faster as I would be back to work and not focusing all day long on him. Wasn't I a bit old to be so wrapped up in someone I hardly knew? I felt like a teeny bopper in love for the first time.

Late in the afternoon of January 7th, walking home from work, I checked my mail box. It was jammed! There were so many postcards that the mailman had put an elastic band around them. I couldn't get into my apartment fast enough; certainly he hadn't written all of these if he was disinterested. He had written more than one a day! It took a few minutes to sort them by date; I wanted to read them sequentially to get the full picture. He was having fun but he was also missing me. He mentioned that he had been told by his father to put away my photograph as company was coming and embarrassing questions could be asked.

What more could I want? I now had proof that Joshua was alive and well and still interested in me: at least interested enough to want to write to me every day. It had been a long time since I felt good about myself and about life. This renewed hope was just what I needed. I pondered the irony of it, meeting someone at the age of 39. I recalled a clairvoyant that I had met in Edmonton in 1975 who told me that my love life would be very rough, and that I would be in my late thirties before I would meet my soulmate. Was Joshua this person?

8

Postcards from Florida

I hadn't expected Josh's postcards to arrive quickly knowing that regular mail during the holidays is typically quite slow and would have been crazy to think that I would be getting any news from him before Boxing Day. When the telephone ran early Christmas morning, I assumed that it was either my sister Claire or one of my brothers calling. Since the conversation was short and cordial, it made me think that he would have made the call within earshot of either his Mom or Dad. He mentioned that he had been writing every day: he intended to mail a first batch of cards as soon as the United States Post Office reopened after the holidays.

Joshua had held to his promise of one postcard a day on which he duly noted the daily temperature as if to remind himself of the reason why he was in Florida. A picture of the Art Deco District of Miami Beach was the first postcard he penned on December 22nd in which he tells of a long second day on the road. Instead of the usual two and half days of travel, they drove all the way to Sunny Isles arriving at 11 pm on that day. He had carefully selected the Art Deco card to please me.

He mentions that while at Pedro's South of the Border, he found a 3 foot sculpture of Michelangelo's David, in one of the gift shops. Fearing his parent's disapproval, he decided not to buy it which was probably a wise decision. Any art featuring naked men would certainly raise eyebrows and would not be condoned. He would have to wait for the day when he lived away from home to acquire such things.

If I had any doubts about his intentions, they were laid to rest with the last four words which read 'I miss you already!'. However, it took until January 6th for the first postcard to arrive in my mailbox. Since our last visit together, my spirits were up and down like a yo-yo. One minute I felt like I had won the lottery, and the next I had mixed emotions. Did I really deserve him? Was this really happening?

The second card was quite ordinary. Intended for visitors to Florida who enjoy teasing, it stated "I've got it nice…while you're having ice!' It was written on December 23rd but only mailed on January 4th as the postmark indicated. It arrived on January 6th and tells about a special outing to celebrate his Dad's 51st birthday.

He signed the two first two postcards 'Joshua'; all others were signed 'Josh'. While we were together, he had never used the abbreviated form of his name; I wondered if this familiarity was a sign that he felt more comfortable with me. Was he in fact letting me see the real person behind the persona?

On January 7th several postcards arrived at once! For the most part, the messages were about daily household chores, trips to the beach to check out the beautiful men and either going out for dinner or having family friends in for a meal. On December 24th and 25th, he wrote two postcards. In one of them, he talks about going to the beach and seeing all the beautiful bodies. 'I'm like a guy on a diet,' he writes, 'I'm content to only look at the menu.' Joshua bemoaned the fact that he was by himself while most people were in couples.

The December 26th card was a view of Key West, although Joshua had never been there. The photograph was taken from the air looking down to the cruise ship dock where a Holland America vessel was tied up. Comparing Key West to Provincetown and San Francisco as one of the major gay Meccas, Joshua revealed that he would like to visit this 'paradise for gay men'.

The other postcard of the same date said something about his concern for mankind. 'It's a common sight to see people standing on the road side with signs to the effect that they would be happy to work for food,' wrote Josh. 'Did you know that at least 20% of the homeless who work don't earn enough money to have a place to sleep? This is Miami today.' Like the petals of a flower that unfurls its beauty each passing day, Joshua was beginning to show me who he really was. Although his family had money, he felt the pain of those less fortunate than himself. At school, after Christmas, when the teacher would ask the students to describe their gifts, Joshua would listen to what all the boys had gotten so that when his turn came he could pretend that he got the same things when in fact, he got a lot more gifts many of which were quite unusual. It would have been easy to flaunt the family wealth but he chose not to do so; few boys his age were as lucky as he was and there was no point in making others feel inferior.

On New Year's Eve, Joshua and his Dad decided to go to Peaches. With a logo that reads 'lot of store, a lot of music', they bought music CDs and books on the disco era. Joshua had said that he enjoyed disco music. What I did not know at the time was that collecting music is his main passion. He collects dance music of the seventies; his collection was and still is very impressive, and was expanded with every visit to a Peaches music store.

In his New Year's Day postcard, Joshua writes about calling his grandmother to wish her a healthy and prosperous New Year. Her wish for him was that he would find a nice young girl to which he responded 'Grandma, why do you wish me trouble?' Either she hadn't clued in to the fact that he was gay or she was fishing to find out. Joshua kept his cards close to his chest for fear that such a revelation might cause heartache. It was way too early to mention that he had met someone he thought would make an excellent life partner. There were some gay relatives on that side of the family; surely there would be acceptance but there was no rush to make an announcement, and certainly not over the phone. Did one really need to tell elderly grandparents about such things? Would it change how they felt about him? He wasn't ready yet to stick his neck out; caution had been drilled into him since his early childhood. For every decision he made, he analyzed the potential for error or problems. Without any sure benefits, he would choose the status quo.

Josh's father took a flight back to Ottawa on January 7th as he needed to be in town for meetings before the week was out. After dropping him off at the Fort Lauderdale airport, Joshua and his mother drove back to the condo where they sat and watched 'Peggy Sue Got Married' for the third time. This 1986 Francis Ford Coppola flick considered by Siskel and Ebert as one of the year's best movies, is about a woman (Peggy Sue Bodell) on the verge of divorce who finds herself transported back to her high school senior years. This romantic fantasy comedy centers on the difficult relationship between Peggy Sue and her husband Charlie who, thanks to the high school reunion, rediscover each other after having come very close to a divorce. Joshua admitted that he had tears in eyes while watching the movie for the third time. He felt nostalgic that evening; he was anxious to return to Canada.

In his last postcard dated January 9th, 1992, Joshua states 'I'm anxious to come back home; I know that you are waiting patiently for my return.'

9

Freedom at Last

'I arrived in Ottawa on Monday, April 26, 1976,' I said. 'I felt a sense of freedom I had never had before. My university years were over; it was time to build a life for myself although I knew it would be quite a while before things would start to fall into place. It would have been very different if Norman and Marcello had not been so welcoming. They made me feel safe, offered me full access to their home and even helped me find temporary employment so that I could make ends meet. In the first years of my life in the Nation's Capital, earning enough money to get by was my main concern.'

'You arrived here without any savings!' said Josh.

From a well-established family with deep pockets, it was difficult for him to comprehend how day-to-day living for someone coming out of university with debt could be the driving force to succeed despite all odds. My parents simply did not have the means to put me through university let alone help me get settled once I graduated.

Here I was living in Old Chelsea, Québec, and a mere twenty-minute drive to downtown Ottawa. The accommodations I shared with Norman and Marcello were spacious and adequate. Located above a rural grocery store run by a young couple struggling to make a go of it, we were within walking distance to the entrance of the Gatineau Park where Café Luigi's was located. This quaint and rustic Italian restaurant was the brainchild of the McCraig family; the second in a small chain of restaurants. It was also where Marcello worked as a bartender and Norman as a waiter. The interior of the restaurant consisted of the entrance vestibule leading directly into the bar to the left and the main dining lounge straight ahead. A smaller dining room was located at the rear of the establishment down a long corridor.

A stone's throw from the village, Café Luigi's had earned an impressive reputation and had a long list of loyal devotees. Nestled in a wooded area and built out of a very old country house not far from the intersection of Kingsmere Road and Notch Road, the restaurant was adjacent to the Dunderosa Golf Course. On hot summer evenings, a cool breeze and the smell of pine from the woods made the property extremely appealing.

The owners had wanted to hire a hostess or greeter who would also take care of the cash. A good word was put forward on my behalf and I was hired without much effort on my part. My title was *Maître d'* and I enjoyed the role and status it gave me. My services were required every evening from Thursday to Sunday. A fair system of sharing gratuities had been established long before I was hired. Because of it, my earnings were decent and allowed me to contribute towards the costs of the food and rent of my hosts.

Luigi's was a very popular restaurant at the time. The décor was old world barn style with soft dim lighting. The burlap-covered walls were decorated with inexpensive but beautiful art, and overhanging lights created a romantic mood carefully designed by the owners. They had chosen dark-stained heavy wood tables with impressive and massive supports. Even the smallest of tables had enormous cross legs supporting the twenty inch square table top. Crooner music had been recorded on reel-to-reel tapes piped in from the McCraig's private accommodations to the restaurant. Mrs. McCraig closely guarded her secret recipes for lasagna, manicotti, crepes cannelloni, and veal parmigiana that had made the restaurant famous.

'Please follow me to the reception area,' Norman said to guests who were about to leave, 'and the *Maître d'* will take care of you.'

After they had paid and left the restaurant, Norman said out loud, *Maître d'* my foot! More like a cashier to me!'

He laughed as he walked away in the direction of the kitchen to pick up his next order. He was right. Although my title was Maître d', I did not perform the usual functions of a person in this position. My sole responsibilities were to greet the guests, hang their coats and jackets and then bring them to their table. When the bills were ready, I would add the applicable taxes and calculate the total. Norman was right; I was a *Maître d'* in name only.

After all the guests had left the restaurant, the staff members would sit together in the small dining room and talk about the high points of the evening. We shared funny anecdotes and divided the tips. Norman always had the best and funniest story.

'I was walking by table 11 when I overhead the conversation of the two elderly ladies sharing a meal,' said Norman. 'One lady asked the other — *Do you have anything between your two legs?* And the second lady answered — *I believe that's none of your business!* The smirk on Norman's face was priceless.'

On Saturday nights, we'd plan a get-together either in our apartment or at a local watering hole. We'd get into bed by 3 or 4 in the morning in the hope that we would not be awakened by the owner's wife singing ABBA tunes along with the radio while she was stocking shelves in the market below us. Disco fever was at its peak and the gay community was lapping it all up. Thanks to us, people like Donna Summer, Vicky Sue Robinson, Van McCoy and many more became super stars. Gays worshipped the disco divas; they bought their music, they danced to it in Discos and followed them from city to city wherever they performed.

Josh, a music aficionado, likes the disco era more than any other period of music. He is interested in hearing how the music of the seventies graced our lives. He is fascinated by any story that includes a mention of the music of his teenage years which had a lasting impression on him. In his opinion, it was the best dance music of all time. He and his sister learned some of the more popular dance routines such as the 'Hustle'.

'I think I've talked enough,' I said. 'I'm afraid of boring you to death.'

'No,' said Josh, 'your stories are captivating. Let's drive up there sometime soon.'

10

A Happy Reunion

The telephone rang early Saturday morning on January 11th, 1992. Could it be him? Was Joshua back in town? I paused not knowing if I should answer. If I answered and it wasn't him, I would be devastated. Oh you silly queen! I thought to myself.

Excitement and fear came over me as I decided that it was silly not to answer the telephone. This was not a case of getting sick over a break up. The butterflies would soon pass and I would know where I stood with Joshua if indeed it was him at the other end of the line.

'Hello,' I said answering the call.

'Richard, this is Joanna calling from the Ottawa Airport Authority. Would you be available to do a shift at the Arrivals desk tomorrow morning?' asked the Volunteer Coordinator.

Hesitating for a moment, I answered, 'Yes, by all means'.

Not wanting to take away any free time that I might have to spend with Joshua had made me dither about doing an extra volunteer shift at the Ottawa Macdonald Cartier International Airport. I really enjoyed working at the Information kiosk at the Arrivals desk. My regular shift had always been Sunday mornings from 9 am to noon. Some people go to church on Sundays; I went to the airport to help others. It was my way of giving back to society. The notion of 'what goes around comes around' made me want to do as much good as possible. How could one possibly lose when trying to be good?

Just as I was about to sit down to write my list of to-do items for the day, the telephone rang again. I answered without any hesitation.

'Hi it's me. I'm back from Florida,' said Josh. 'I've got so much to tell you about our trip. Do you have time to meet me?' he said.

'Can you come to dinner this evening?' I asked with a broad grin as though he could see me from the other end of the line.

'That would be perfect,' replied Josh. 'I really missed you; I'm anxious to see you again. I can stay overnight if that's OK with you.'

I wanted to say 'You can stay as long as you want' but thought that would be coming on too strong. We had taken quite a liking to each other but were we really compatible? How many of my friends had rushed into relationships too quickly only to have to pull back when they realized that the person they thought they knew well turned out to be very different from their initial assessment.

'Sure Josh,' I said. 'That will give us plenty of time to get caught up. I want to hear all the details of your time in Sunny Isles. I bet you're tanned all over!'

'My Dad's condo is right next to Haulover Beach where there is a nudist section but I'd get killed if I went there in my birthday suit,' said Joshua, laughing as the words came out of his mouth.

'I'll expect you late afternoon' I said. 'Remember not to park too close to the fence otherwise Tony will have problems removing the snow should we get another 4 to 6 centimeters of the white stuff.'

'Ok, see you later,' Joshua said as he ended the conversation and hung up.

Making meals for one was one thing but preparing a succulent dish to impress was a different matter. I had not enquired about allergies and food intolerances. What was I thinking! Should I call back and ask? I realized that I didn't have his telephone number. Even if I did, would I risk calling and getting one of his parents on the line? Would they associate the voice with the face in the picture on Josh's night table in Florida? Would they think I'm too old for their son?

So many questions filled my mind; I feared losing it. What was the point of worrying about this at this time? *Focus on dinner you fool*, I thought trying to free myself from self-doubt and unjustifiable fears.

Eventually settling for a chicken casserole, this easy-to-make dish would be ideal as it would allow us to spend all of our time together and avoid the kitchen to the greatest extent. I would prepare it ahead of time and put it in the oven at 4:30 so that the smell of the meal would permeate the apartment.

At five pm, the intercom buzzer sounded indicating Josh's arrival. I opened the apartment door and there he was smiling as I had remembered him. He took one step into the apartment and immediately hugged me. That reassured me in a way I hadn't felt since we saw last each other in mid-December. There's nothing fake about him; he was natural and exuberant. He disliked phony people; he had no use for them. It was evident that he was authentic and expected others to be as well.

'Come and tell me all about Florida. How was the trip down? I want to hear about it,' I said.

'We left on December 21st so that we would be in Florida in time for my Dad's birthday,' Joshua said. 'My Mom always makes sure that we do something special for my Dad as his birthday is so close to Christmas. When he was young, he hated the fact that he had been born on December 23rd. He'd get one gift that covered both his birthday and Christmas. I guess he felt that it was a bit unfair.'

'Did you make it on time?' I enquired.

'Yes,' Joshua replied. 'We drove from Ottawa to the US border crossing at the Thousand Islands Bridge. After entering the United States, the snow and wind made for difficult driving particularly just north of Syracuse, New York near Parish. Lake-effect snow is a problem there every time we drive through. Once we got south of Syracuse, the roads were much better; we did good time getting into Fredericksburg, Virginia, our first stopover, arriving at about 5 pm.'

'Is that north or south of Washington?' I asked.

'It's due south of Washington on Highway 17 at the junction of Highway 95 which takes us all the way to Florida,' said Josh. 'It's an easy place to get in and out; moreover, there are so many hotels that it is easy to find lodging. We typically take two and a half days to get to Florida. Normally our second night is in northern Florida near St. Augustine leaving us just an easy drive on the third and final day.'

'I've never traveled that far by car. It must get boring at times. Is it scenic?' I enquired.

'Although it is highway driving most of the way, I enjoy the scenery, the small towns and a few special places where my Dad likes to stop and walk around,' Joshua said.

'Give me an example of such a place,' I said.

'Pedro's South of the Border,' said Josh. 'This place is very unusual. Before you come to it, you see signs from as far as 100 miles advertising it. Each billboard is different; the eye-catching advertisements are delightful and amusing. Pedro's is within five miles of the border that separates North and South Carolina. It started with a gas station and a restaurant; every year they add a new pavilion, a store, an amusement ride, a car wash, or something else that may attract people to the site. All the buildings are painted in vibrant colors reminiscent of Mexico. It's tasteless but it can be a feast for the eyes. We seldom drive by without stopping; it's become a tradition. In the center of this bizarre cluster of buildings is a tall pointed tower on which sits an enormous multi-colored sombrero. It's the epitome of kitsch!'

'Do you stop for meals?' I asked.

'My mother packs the cooler so that we have plenty of food while in transit; however, we eat out every night,' said Josh.

'Speaking of eating, I should get supper on the table,' I said.

Later that evening, Joshua admitted that he was rather fond of me and that he'd like to see me on a regular basis. At his suggestion, we would meet once during the week and spend our weekends together provided his parents hadn't lined up chores for him to do in which case he would try to get all tasks done during the week so that he'd have his weekends free. This was more than I expected; going along with this plan meant that we would see each on a regular basis and on my turf which would make it easier for me.

After the meal, Joshua joined me in the kitchen to help with the dishes. Always there to help when needed, he dried the dishes and put them away. His mother had done a great job of raising him and showing him how to do household chores.

When the work was done, we sat down in the living room to chat. The conversation led into the same direction as last time. Joshua would enquire about my early years in Ottawa, the friends I had, the places I had lived in and the jobs that I had held. Although I had already told him a lot about me, he wanted more. He was curious about how I felt going through difficult times such as the AIDS epidemic, losing close friends, finding accommodations in a city where good and affordable rental units were rare. It was difficult for him to understand how I could live so far from my immediate family. I shared with him things I had withheld from everyone else. My gut feeling was that I could trust him with my innermost secrets and knowing that he would respect my privacy and not divulge intimate information that I shared with him.

11

Looking for a Purpose

Thoughts of my brother lying in a Montreal hospital clinging to life with all the force he was able to muster had occupied my mind so much so that I hadn't been able to see the interest that anyone else could have for me. When Joshua first appeared in my surroundings, I was completely oblivious to him. On the second occasion, I took notice but I was not in a frame of mind to realize that he wanted to meet me. So preoccupied was I with my brother's struggles that had he not been persistent, we would not have met. Absent such determination, our paths would not have crossed; any chance of building a relationship would have been irretrievably lost. It baffled me that Joshua never gave up; it was a sign of a person who was willing to try and try again when initial success was elusive. Who was this unusual person? Why was he so intent in meeting someone as ordinary as I?

My brother Geoffrey's illness gave rise to feelings of inferiority that I had harbored all of my life. He was the closest in age and resembled me the most of all my other siblings. Good looking and popular with everyone, he made friends easily. He was everything that I wasn't; I felt that he had it all and that I had made a mess of my life. His near rock-star status as a drummer in one of the local bands gave him the notoriety and small-town fame that I could only dream of achieving. Yet, my one and only desire was to leave Dodge without destroying my reputation or that of the Steeves family, as having a queer son is not something a family would be proud of. My dark past was never far from me; in a large city like Ottawa, I could let go of the past but I could not forget the feelings of shame that I felt for not being the perfect son that my parents may have wanted. To succeed in a large city, one must have nerves of steel and tons of confidence; I had neither but I had a strong will to make a name for myself. Maybe it was this underlying motivation that Joshua saw in me.

A few months before meeting Josh, I met three nice guys; James, a deacon from Manitoba, Paul, a priest from London and Tom, a theology student at the London Seminary. Our discussions about the Church fueled my repressed desires of becoming a priest that had sprung up while I was a student in a junior seminary in New Brunswick in the 1960s. All three were gay; however, that did not seem to be an issue for them. They felt that they could follow the Church's teachings, in spite of the fact that homosexuality was frowned upon by the Vatican. It appeared that as long as one didn't flaunt one's sexuality, the church hierarchy would turn a blind eye. For years, I had contemplated the priesthood, thinking that serving God would give meaning to my life. However, I could not accept the Catholic Church's position on homosexuality, let alone being a gay priest and having a partner on the side. Parallel lives were unfair to each partner. I had no intentions of living a lie; honesty and truthfulness were the cornerstones of my being.

My fears of growing old alone intensified as the years wore on. At 39, I was neither the most attractive guy nor the most appealing person in any crowd. I was drawn to people who were primarily young, attractive and self-assured. On the cusp of turning 40, which in the gay world means the start of old age, the pressure to find a mate grows stronger than ever. Chronic arthritis which mostly affected my spine was debilitating, and added years to my life. Pain was a daily occurrence; I managed it as best I could hoping that it would go undetected. Just prior to meeting Josh, I suffered a severe bout of arthritis likely caused by the tensions created at work along with the uncertainty concerning Geoffrey's illness.

In the weeks leading up to my first meeting with Josh, Geoffrey had been transferred from the Hotel Dieu Hospital in Québec City (where he underwent chemotherapy and daily mustard baths) to the Montreal General for radiation therapy after which he was released and continued his treatments with self-administered interferon. During my visits to the Montreal hospital, he admitted to me that he had had night sweats for almost a year; HIV testing was considered but flatly rejected by

Geoffrey. Did he think that they suspected he was gay? He was an exceptional case. Soiled bed sheets were not reused, they had to be destroyed as a precautionary measure. According to the medical team attending to him, there were only a handful of similar cases at any one time in the province of Québec.

I took strength wherever I could find it. I read to keep occupied and to get my mind away from negative thoughts. In *A New Day; 365 Meditations for Personal and Spiritual Growth*, by J.S. Dorian, the following quote stopped me right in my tracks:

There are times when we face especially difficult tasks. When we contemplate the enormity of what lies ahead, our projections often tell us that we can't possibly make it through — even though we must. We become so thoroughly persuaded we're going to fall short, that our negative conviction becomes a self-fulfilling prophesy.

Everywhere I looked, there were positive signs: messages of hope I could not ignore. Walking along Elgin Street, at the corner of Somerset Street in front of St John the Evangelist Church, the daily message board read: 'You were carried in at birth and you will be carried out at your death. How about walking in the interval?' Despite my arthritis, I could walk; I would continue to stand and make the best of what life had given me. Would Josh's presence alter the course of my life? Would he give it meaning?

My brother Phil's wife, Janice, a nurse by profession, had stated that it was likely that Geoffrey would be gone by Christmas, his situation had deteriorated so quickly. Fearing that he would pass before I had a chance to reconcile my differences with him, I made peace with Geoffrey on my last visit at the Montreal General just a few days before Christmas, but the holidays had come and gone, and my brother was back in his home in Campbellton. He had beaten the odds; he would be around much longer than even the most optimistic person had predicted.

Now that Geoffrey was back home, I was able to get on with my own life. It was clear that he wasn't cured but the remission gave him time to tie loose ends and prepare for the inevitable. Serene throughout the weeks and months that followed, his partner, Gisèle, cared and nursed him around the clock. His flaking skin left trails of white particles wherever he went; bed linens had to be changed every other day and washed in very hot water with large amounts of bleach. That he always smiled throughout this ordeal was a mystery to me; he was certainly blessed with an inner strength that had not been observed before. I marveled at his ability to be positive when all things appeared so gloomy. I had nothing to complain about; seeing Geoffrey this way was a great lesson in life: accept gracefully what the Lord has given you and make the best of it.

12

The Start of a Relationship

True to his word and exactly as planned, Joshua was back in Ottawa on January 10th. The next morning, he called keeping the conversation short and to the point. He missed me; he wanted to know when we could get together. To me, this was reassuring; a whole new world was ours to discover, to create. Through everyday living, we would learn about each other while building a relationship slowly, carefully and thoughtfully. I had learned from past experience; I would not make the same mistakes twice. There is no urgency to developing relationships.

Joshua and I planned to spend the weekend together to continue where we had left off just prior to his departure for the United States. My plan was to bring him up to date on all the family news which included Phil's imminent separation from his wife Janice, my youngest brother Danny's plans to wed Marianne, the latest on Geoffrey's condition and my father's failing health. It must have sounded like a soap opera. However, Joshua was hearing about my siblings in details I had not revealed before. Politely, he asked questions to clarify, and to get additional information to complete the partial stories I was telling him. Never once did I feel that he was making judgments on what I was saying or on the lives of the people I spoke about.

Wedding plans were also being discussed in Josh's family; his only sister Louisa was getting married in the spring. Aware that Joshua was seeing someone, she made it clear that he alone was invited to her wedding. Even if he had been given the opportunity to be accompanied, he would not have asked me to join him. It was far too early in the relationship to risk alienating family members. After all, he was part of a very small tight-knit family where outsiders were not easily welcomed.

His father, the Member of Parliament for Gatineau, had an impeccable reputation; it was best to avoid anything that could have a negative impact on his standing and stature. A man of strong character, he made his positions clear to the citizens of Gatineau. He was well-liked and well-respected for all the good work he had done to attract business to the town. Residents came directly to him with their concerns; he helped each one individually, resolving long-standing problems.

One issue that wasn't so easy for his father to deal with was perhaps Josh's homosexuality. The source of his discomfort was unclear. As a politician in the 1990s, having a gay son was not anything that would help bolster his image. Like a gray cloud looming high in the sky, the possibility of not having grandchildren preyed on his mind. Various options to resolve Joshua's defect were offered, and they included therapy sessions, services of a prostitute or anything else that could help him appreciate women and forget about men.

Joshua was steadfast in his position to remain true to himself. He would not allow his father to dictate to him how he should feel, who he should date and who he should befriend. My picture discovered by chance on Josh's night table in the condo in Florida had done nothing to appease the concerns of a father and a politician who did everything to keep the press out of his personal affairs. Joshua conveyed to me his father's concerns in a way that made me think that it would take nothing less than a miracle for our relationship to be accepted by his family. I sensed that it would be a long haul before we could be seen together in public in Gatineau.

O'Connor Street was on this side, across the river, and in a different city where Joshua was not well known. By spending time in my apartment, we could avoid prying eyes; we could stay under the radar, hoping that time would help resolve the unpleasantness of not being able to be completely in the open. Joshua was not as afraid as I was of appearing in public in Ottawa nor was he shy about being seen with a man 10 years his senior.

In January of 1992, we planned a few outings: one to the Ottawa Film Club and another to the Ottawa Lambda supper meeting where Josephine Holitzner, the city mayor, had been invited as a guest speaker. It was hard to tell who got the most attention Josephine or Josh. As one of the Lambda Executive, I was well known to regular members who always saw me alone at the meetings. That evening, quite a few guys came up to me to be introduced to the dashing young man sitting to my left.

Once the guest speaker had finished her short talk, she took questions from the floor. A variety of issues were raised, most of which centered on the city's ability and desire to serve the growing gay population of Ottawa to which the mayor responded positively and with great enthusiasm. She was known as being gay-positive, and while not flaunting the gay agenda, would certainly help move things in the right direction and in our favor. No promises were made lest she went for re-election without having accomplished much to help the gay community.

It didn't take long before we felt the effects of Mayor Holitzner's presentation at the Lambda function. Josh's father told him that he was upset because of his involvement in the gay movement. Apparently, members of the Gatineau press had called Josh's father to enquire on where he stood with respect to gay rights. A few days later, an article in the Ottawa Citizen discussed the position on gay rights taken by several elected officials from nearby cities. Before his parents left on a two week holiday to Florida, Joshua gave them a copy of the book 'I've got something to tell you', in which is explained in simple terms what homosexuality is and suggests ways of dealing with coming-out issues.

The time had come for Joshua to meet some of my friends. I introduced him to Mary Pointer who had been my pillar of support in the months leading up to my meeting Josh. Mary, a Sagittarius like Josh's Dad, liked him from the moment she met him. In fact, it was mutual. Mary's spunk and frank opinions impressed Josh.

I was eager to have Joshua meet my sister Claire. If he won her approval, I'd feel so much better as she and I have always been very close; she is my only sister and after my mother passed away, she became the *de facto* mother to me. A meeting had been planned in Montréal; Claire was expecting to be there on business but last minute cutbacks at the Public Service Commission put a stop to her travel plans. There would be other occasions, I thought to myself; not to worry, things happen for a reason.

Shortly after arriving in Ottawa, I had taken an interest in all things antique so when a major show in Kanata was announced, I asked Joshua if he would be interested in coming along with me. He did not appear to be very interested in antiques.

'Will there only be old stuff?' said Josh.

'Antiques,' I said, 'not junk. There will be some high-quality furniture, collectibles, memorabilia, and possibly vintage clothing.'

'Why do you want to buy old things when you can buy something new?' enquired Josh.

'For me, some of the old pieces of furniture, china and glass are far more interesting because they have been used and because their designs are a lot more original than what we find in stores today.' I replied.

'Do you think someone will be selling old records?' asked Josh.

'Every show I've been to, there is always at least one vendor who is trying to sell old 78s, 45s and LPs,' I commented.

'Now you've got me interested,' said Josh. 'Let's go!'

It was an eye opener for Joshua to see the variety of merchandize on offer by vendors from all over Ontario and Upper New York State. We came home with an August 1st 1874 copy of Harper's Weekly — A Journal of Civilization with a cover featuring a snapshot entitled 'The College Regatta' in which seven handsome men in full uniform pose together as a team. The magazine was in pristine condition; it had been kept by a collector whose origins were unknown to the seller. Joshua had spotted it and, hoping that I would like it as much as he did, was eager to buy it. He wanted to display it in my apartment as though we had purchased it together for our mutual enjoyment. Once framed, it was given a prominent place in our living room. We considered it our first joint possession, a sign that we were starting to cocoon.

Before I met Josh, he had been dating Mark Lafontaine. However, that relationship ended in the fall of 1991 even though they remained good friends. I felt indebted to Mark for having originally introduced us, although I had very little recollection of that event. Mark had since met Peter Gardner and together they seemed like the perfect couple. We decided to invite them to dinner so that we could get to know Peter. What could have been a very quiet meal turned out to be a delightful gathering with plenty of laughter and story telling. Joshua and Peter hit it off very well, being similar in many ways. They shared the same twisted sense of humor. I was seeing a playful Joshua whose interactions with Mark and Peter were courteous, respectful and spontaneous. By now, I had observed him in various situations and, in each one, he came across as a mature, well-balanced and gentle man. He was a keeper and I knew it!

13

A Sunday Afternoon Surprise

Joshua never tired of hearing me talk about my early days in Ottawa. He was curious about my background but he was equally fascinated by what had happened in the years before we knew each other. Each time we met, I told a bit more about my trials and tribulations of past years. I worried that all of this information might scare him away; he might all of sudden realize that I had a chequered past, that I had been a slut. I would have to tell him about the many relationships I had had before meeting him. Some were long, others were short. Rejection had been a two-way street. I had been rejected by more than one person but I too had rejected guys who I felt could not be life-long partners. Interesting and attractive as some were, I realized that it takes a lot more than just good sex and common interests to make a relationship work. A soulmate was what I looking for, although at the time I don't think I knew exactly how to define it.

Just as I started to think that things would get easier for a while, my life took an unexpected turn. Back in the fall of 1977, on the invitation of a friend who had just moved to the Nation's Capital from Moncton, I agreed to share a two bedroom apartment in Hull. Dave McConnell was what one would describe as a tall bear. Overweight, hairy, and over 6 feet, his 230 pound frame appeared enormous to me, yet he was as gentle as a lamb; he wouldn't hurt a fly.

Place Radisson had just been built; the complex included half a dozen buildings on a large piece of land close to the expressway. It was largely vacant when we decided to take residence on the 7th floor of 4 Place Radisson. A western sunlight flooded all of the rooms providing an added pleasure I hadn't expected when we signed the lease. From our balcony, we had stunning views of downtown Ottawa including the Parliament Buildings.

Dave had been married; he had since separated from his wife although they were still on very good terms. After separating the assets in a fair manner, Dave was left with enough furniture to establish himself in a new place. I, on the other hand, had no furniture at all. Other than my clothes, my books and my stereo system, my money had been used to buy an old wine-colored Pontiac Parisienne. For a mere $500, I acquired a clunker that was good enough to get me to the gay hotspots in Hull, across the river.

On a cold Sunday afternoon of February 13th, 1977, Dave and I had decided to take a nap. The skies were grey and the air nippy; the damp chill just wanted to make you curl up and sleep, which is what we did. An alarm sounded in the distance; it woke me up. Thinking that it was Dave's alarm clock, I turned over to go back to sleep. Dave did the same, thinking that it was my clock radio that had gone off. However, after a few minutes, the alarm annoyed him enough that he got up to ask me to 'shut the damn thing off'. It was then that he realized that the noise was coming from the hallway. He opened the apartment door; the stench of smoke was unmistakable. We had to get out.

'Rich, get up! We've got to vacate the building,' said Dave.

'What's happening?' I said.

'There's smoke in the hallways; we need to get out of here fast.' added Dave. 'Get dressed, take what you need and let's get the hell out of here.'

Within seconds, we were ready to leave having each taken something we did not want to lose or something we thought we would need. I followed Dave down the hallway to the south end of the building. As we descended the stairwell, the smoke got thicker: more and more people gathered as the lower floors were emptying. By the time we reached the third floor, it was impossible to see where we were going; people were crying out loud. There were many people gathered at the exit making sure that we were fine.

Fire had engulfed the north end of the second floor; the flames were shooting out of a window halfway down the corridor. From the conversations we overhead, it appeared that the second floor was being used as a temporary shelter for seniors who were waiting for a health care home to be built. A cigarette lit by an older gentleman in unit 207 had ignited the mattress. An attendant on duty opened the unit door causing the oxygen to fuel the fire and set the whole room ablaze; he died instantly. I had never come so close to death; it shook me to the core.

'What did you take away from the apartment? I asked Dave. He looked at me, put his hands in his pockets and took out two apples.

'Fat people need to eat!' replied Dave. 'I'm always afraid I'll be hungry. Food takes precedence in my order of priorities. What did you save?'

'My contact lenses,' I said. 'Other than my car, these are the most expensive things I own.'

We laughed at how different we were from each other. Our values were diametrically opposed; we were both from New Brunswick but from very different backgrounds. We connected on many levels and we knew many of the gay guys in Moncton. After the clean-up had been completed, we were allowed back into the building but I did not feel safe. The unmistakable smell of smoke lingered for weeks. And so did my sad feelings. I wondered to what extent we were safe. A man had died due to the carelessness of a smoker. I decided it was time to find alternate accommodations knowing that this experience would follow me for the rest of my life.

Career wise, my first break came in May of 1977 when I was offered a job to replace a second-language teacher at the Gatineau Elementary School on Maple Street. Oddly enough, the town of Gatineau had been started by the Canadian International Paper (CIP) Company, the same company that owned the paper mill in Dalhousie, my hometown. The school erected just across from the Post Office had been commissioned to serve the children of workers at the paper mill. The residences built on streets that bore names such as Poplar, Birch and Cypress, were CIP-designed houses identical to those I had seen in Dalhousie as a child. This familiarity made me feel at home in this Anglo-Saxon district of the town that had been originally called Gatineau Mills.

My Mother had not influenced me in any way to enter the teaching profession yet I felt drawn to it. She had a passion for teaching, also knew how hard it was and the efforts needed to become a seasoned teacher. The long hours with few rewards were not for the faint of heart. Teaching paid well but if you got hooked by the above-average salaries, you would end up staying in the profession without really liking it.

I needed the money so I took the two month assignment thinking that at the end of it, I would find another job. Just prior to the end of the school year, the Protestant School Board of Western Québec enquired about my interest in signing a one year contract. Teaching French as a second language to Kindergarten and Grades 1 to 3 wasn't my idea of a dream job but it would pay the bills and more; it also gave me the chance to start a more stable period of my life. Gatineau would become a place near and dear to my heart. At the time, I had no idea that I would eventually meet someone special from that town.

What was in store for me was a mystery. There were so many surprises and unexpected happenings; snow had fallen in Miami and in the Bahamas in January, the only time in history. I had no inkling that I would have a connection to Miami.

Saturday Night Fever starring John Travolta had opened in New York City. It helped popularize disco music around the world. The film showcased the music, the dancing and the subculture surrounding the disco era: symphony-orchestrated melodies, graceful choreography, haute couture and pre-AIDS sexual promiscuity. AIDS would eventually have a larger-than-life impact on the world. In another 5 to 7 years, my life would be consumed with this terminal disease, something so big and ominous that it scared the living daylights out of me.

14

Planning for Europe

Movies were a common interest; any good motion picture was reason enough for Joshua and I to get together for a night out. On the way out of the theatre after seeing 'Green Fried Tomatoes', we talked about the significance of same-sex relationships and the difficulty of telling others about it. Based on a book entitled 'Green Fried Tomatoes at the Whistle Stop Café', the filmmakers drew criticism from some reviewers for removing the lesbian angle in the book's plot, but the film won a GLADD Media Award for "best lesbian content".

'Coming out is never easy,' said Josh. 'Wouldn't it be nice if we didn't have to?'

'Are you implying that you are still having problems with your parents?' I enquired.

'Not so much a problem of accepting me as a homosexual but rather the stigmatization of what they believe two men do together. I think they see homosexuality as a sickening perversion,' said Josh. 'I'm concerned about what they think; however, I don't believe that they would attempt to stop our relationship. My Mother is far more accepting of homosexuality than my Father who, in his own way, cannot see how two people of the same sex could possibly be attracted to each other. More importantly for him is how others in the community will react on hearing the news.'

'Guess it will be a long time before I get invited to your parents' home,' I said.

'I didn't want to tell you this, but my Father said that you will never set foot in his house while he's alive,' Joshua said sadly.

Changing the subject, we talked about our plans for the trip to Europe. We agreed on all the major places we wanted to visit, on the length of the trip and on minimum accommodation requirements. It was decided that we would fly to Amsterdam and rent a car. I assumed that since we both had an international driver's license we would share the driving.

We saw this trip as a test of our relationship. Being together 24 hours a day, seven days a week could be a lot more difficult than simply spending weekends together. Would we get on each other's nerves? The one-month odyssey would certainly bring to light any issues that could potentially make it difficult for us to cohabit. I had never shared accommodations with a partner; Joshua was still living at home. There was a tacit agreement that if we could pull this off without a hitch, living together would certainly be possible.

Is one ever ready to give up living alone to risk sharing a home with a partner? Any bachelor will tell you that one gets set in one's ways; changing patterns is difficult at the best of times. I had wanted a partner badly but I hadn't thought it through; I hadn't really put much thought into the idea that I might consider sharing my apartment. It reflected who I was; I decorated it to my taste and displayed my collections of glass and china. My taste in furnishings was rather eclectic and included antiques and ultra modern pieces blended together to create a sophisticated look. My interior design courses came in handy; I had developed a decorating style that my friends called 'shabby chic'. With a limited budget and few resources, I had to make the best of what I could afford. Having an eye for good design and great bargains, I acquired a hodge-podge of furniture and accessories that became my palette to create stunning interiors. I challenged myself to redesign the living room every 4-6 months or whenever I acquired a new piece that had to be included in a room. Even though Joshua liked the apartment, would he feel comfortable in someone else's surroundings? I was worried that he would not feel at home; I was also apprehensive about making significant changes to accommodate his tastes.

Fear of the unknown always bothered me; I was never comfortable not knowing how things would unfold. Worry was my middle name. Not being able to clearly see down the road was probably at the root of my bouts of uveitis — inflammation of the uvea, linked to my arthritis (Ankylosingspondylitis — inflammation of the spine), I had my second major attack in February of 1992. Not as severe as the first one, it nonetheless put me out of commission for a few days. Thinking at first that it was 'pink eye', I was slow to react and get help. Visits to the Eye Clinic at the Ottawa General became a regular occurrence as I tried to reduce the inflammation with steroid drops which had to be closely monitored by eye specialists. Once the inflammation was controlled, then the dosage of the eye drops could be reduced ever so slowly so that the inflammation would not be reignited. I wondered if Joshua would be turned off by my myriad health issues.

Shared passion was going to furniture stores. Josh has an eye for modern and sleek furniture. Antiques, therefore, are not his cup of tea. I had been thinking about purchasing a curio cabinet in which to display my collection of Depression-era glass. An art deco pattern called 'Manhattan' had caught my eye a few years earlier and now I had a huge collection that needed to be appropriately displayed. We came across a huge Italian-made art deco cabinet that was perfect (with the exception of the hefty price tag). I considered selling my bronze whippet hound to help defray the costs. In the end, I kept my bronze and bought the curio on credit. I couldn't part with my dog 'Boo'.

When it was delivered, Joshua helped me decide on the best location in the living room. As always, it meant moving furniture around; this new piece had a huge impact. In the end, we moved furniture in four separate rooms to get everything to fit together. It was then that I noticed that Joshua was very creative in coming up with good design ideas. What was more interesting was the fact that we were doing this work as though we were already living together. This task had served to show us that we were able to work well together, respecting each other's ideas. It forebode well.

I got news that Geoffrey was in Montréal for a check-up; he was doing as well as could be expected under the circumstances. His medications had the desired effect of giving him those extra years he would not have had, had he chosen the path of least resistance. Geoffrey was a fighter; he would never give up easily. This character trait was not obvious when we were living at home as kids. However, he had shown many times over his resilience in the face of unspeakable hardships. I was proud of him in ways I had never imagined. A sense of peace and serenity came over me.

Tranquility was replaced with apprehension as Joshua planned a get-together with his sister Louisa and his co-worker Andrew. My initial reaction to the proposed lunch date quickly changed from apprehension to fear; Louisa would most certainly report back on her observations. Josh's parents would find out about me indirectly. It was at least a step in the right direction regardless of my feelings. This meeting happened just days before Josh's parents were due back in town for a short stay as Josh's Dad went on an unexpected business trip to Asia.

15

A New Dawn
— Remembering Gary & Gerry

Finally, everything was coming together nicely. A regular paycheck afforded me opportunities galore. In October 1978, I bought a canary-yellow Dodge Arrow. With a manual transmission and a sleek black interior, this car made heads turn. I commuted from Hull to the Gatineau Elementary School, a short 25-to-30 minute drive depending on traffic. Having a reliable new vehicle was a luxury for which I had yearned.

Gerry's roommate moved out and I was invited to take his place in a two bedroom ground floor apartment in a small high-rise in Sandy Hill, near the University of Ottawa Campus. It had been my dream to live right downtown. When Gerry made the offer, it didn't take me long to make the decision to leave the apartment I shared with David at Place Radisson. All of my possessions could fit in the back seat of the car with the exception of the box spring and mattress I had acquired since my arrival in the Nation's Capital. Thanks to the kindness of one of Gerry's friends who owned a small truck, I was able to move all of my things in one load with the box spring and mattress crowning the multitude of boxes underneath. On a rainy Thursday evening, we got on the expressway leading into downtown Ottawa via the Macdonald-Cartier Bridge. The truck was right behind me as I led the way in my Dodge Arrow. Driving dangerously slow so that the contents of the truck would not move, we rounded the near-90-degree curve behind 'Les Galeries de Hull' when all of a sudden a gust of wind caught the box spring. From my rear view mirror, I saw it fly up in the air and land in the water-filled ditch. We stopped to see if we could salvage it. Out of the question! I could do without the box spring; the mattress was the more important of the two.

'You have no idea what happened on the way over,' I said. 'I've just polluted the environment in Hull; my box spring is now in a culvert along Highway 5.'

'You might be lucky,' said Gerry with a broad smile. 'Someone just moved out and left a mattress and box spring in the garbage room downstairs. Let's go take a look.'

'If I had lost the mattress, that would be different,' I said. 'But a box spring is a different story. If it's relatively clean, I'll swallow my pride.'

'Take a look,' said Gerry. 'It almost like new. Your mattress will cover it nicely.'

'It will do for now,' I said. 'If it turns out to be uncomfortable, I'll buy a new one.'

For someone I had only known for a few years, Gerry turned out to be a caring and sensitive person, the kind of guy anyone would have wanted as a friend. Cheerful, helpful and discrete, he was gregarious like no other person I knew. There were always people coming in or going out of our apartment. He had made a huge circle of friends since arriving in Ottawa in 1975, a year earlier than me. Generous to a fault, Gerry loved to entertain; humor was central to anything he did and everywhere he went. If he couldn't have fun, there was no point in pursuing it.

Through Gerry, I made many friends and acquaintances. We were invited to parties on a regular basis. In turn, I introduced Gerry to Norman. They hit it off very well. All three of us would get together, smoke a joint and watch *Mary Hartman, Mary Hartman* an American soap opera parody. The show's title was the eponymous character's name stated twice, because Louise Lear, the star of the series, and the writers believed that everything that was said on a soap opera was said twice. It was zany humor the likes of which was best appreciated under the influence of whatever stimulant we could lay our hands on. A bag of Oreos was a must, particularly if we had smoked marijuana, as we would get the munchies.

On a dare made by a colleague at the Gatineau Elementary School, I drove to Syracuse, New York for a long weekend. I had been feeling low; I was getting desperate to meet the man of my dreams. Maybe the Marlborough man lived in or around Syracuse; the only way to find out was to make the short four-hour trip due south of Ottawa. Off I went right after work on Friday afternoon getting into Central New York State just before eight pm. It didn't take me long to find the gay watering hole on South Warren Street where it was easy to meet the locals who had just got off work. I stood at the bar and ordered a beer. Not knowing what was on tap, I asked the bartender what the options were. This gave me away; it was obvious that I was an out-of-towner which brought me much attention.

I noticed three guys standing at the bar not too far from where I was. They were all a bit older than me; I found them attractive and interesting to watch. They were out for a good time; they laughed and prodded each other at every opportunity. One of them, a slightly chubby bearded-bear type, had a broad warm smile. I found him particularly interesting and I could tell that I had caught his eye. Within a half-hour, I was included in their private circle and stood next to Gary Armstrong, an insurance executive, a kind and gentle person not quite as manly as his namesake. The two others guys in this threesome were a couple; I had made the right selection.

Gary and I spend the remainder of the weekend together in his apartment which he shared with a room mate and former partner. The two other guys were the landlords and lived on the first floor of a well kept older home not far from Syracuse University. Gary and his former spouse John had decorated their two-bedroom apartment in a style and using colors that could best be described as manly. Using a chocolate brown, beige and rust combination, the color scheme flowed beautifully from one room to the other. Richly appointed with high-end furniture placed to make the biggest impact, these guys had managed to turn an average apartment into a showpiece. I felt very comfortable in this gorgeous and impeccably clean home.

I had no illusions about the possibility of a long-term relationship with a foreigner. I had no desire to move to the U.S. and Gary certainly was not going to live any further north of Syracuse. In fact, his dream was to move to Florida; he hated winter. I went along for the ride, however short or protracted it would turn out.

Back in Ottawa, Gerry was in no rush to have me vacate the room I had been renting from him. He understood that I wanted my own space so that I could decorate according to my desires and tastes. So when I found a real deal that I couldn't turn down, he was not too upset. It was a stroke of luck that I was the first to see this one-bedroom apartment at the corner of Chapel and Somerset streets. For $182 a month including parking, it was the bargain of the century. The trailer-like apartment needed a lot of TLC to make it a home but with clever decorating skills and know-how, I was convinced that this place was a diamond in the rough. With access to a creepy basement where I was allowed to have a washer, the unit ran the length of the building such that every room had a window, including the bathroom. This south-facing rental was oddly divided. Upon entering, the hall was big enough to accommodate my large glass top dining table. To the left was a smallish bedroom. Down the corridor past the hall was the living room leading into the galley kitchen with breakfast nook near the window. Access to the washroom was from the kitchen which had probably been added long after the original construction and most probably when the building was redesigned into apartments.

I took possession of the apartment on December 22nd and right after the movers had completed their job, I again drove to Syracuse to spend Christmas with Gary. Up until the holidays, Gary had not shared his feelings towards me. He was a hard person to read; I saw no reason to force the issue as it was plain that a cross-border relationship would be difficult if not impossible to sustain over a long period of time. *Never give up* was my motto; he was the best so far and I wasn't about to dump him just because the future was unclear.

On Christmas morning during the gift exchange, the focus was on me. I opened a number of presents; Gary knew that I was moving into my first apartment and that I needed kitchen stuff. A self-taught gourmet cook, Gary had gone out and purchased several functional kitchen items which I appreciated very much. I was overwhelmed by his generosity; I felt his love in a way I hadn't before. Just when I thought we had finished opening gifts, Gary went into the bedroom to retrieve yet another well-wrapped box the contents of which would floor me. Lightweight and impossible to guess its contents, I unwrapped this mysterious offering. Why had he kept it to be opened last? The box was so beautifully wrapped that I did my best not to tear the wrapping paper, and to treasure this special present, a tweed scarf lined with brown silk.

'Do you like it?' asked Gary.

'It's really beautiful,' I said. 'Did you make this?'

'Yes I did,' Gary added. 'However, the coat that goes with it is not yet finished. I had hoped to be done by now but it will take me a few more months.'

'How on earth did you know what size to make the coat?' I said.

'Remember when you borrowed John's jacket when you were here in November?' said Gary. 'I was able to figure out your size based on that coat. I chose brown tweed seeing that you wear that color a lot.'

'I don't know what to say,' I said. 'I have never been given such a generous gift. Thank you, thank you!'

The trip back to Ottawa went by in flash. I kept thinking about Gary; his sewing skills, his decorating skills and his kindness towards me. It would be difficult to reciprocate, not having the financial means to do so. I felt disadvantaged because of my age and my modest income. He was certainly going to move to Florida eventually; I would be left behind. Gary would never be forgotten; few people had been so kindhearted.

16

A Glimpse of the In-Laws

I've always believed that things happen for a reason; whether unexpected or planned, life's little surprises occur to allow us to move forward in some way. What may appear to be a setback can in fact be favorable regardless of how one felt at the time it occurred. The key is recognizing the lessons that can be learned and then moving on.

As the weeks went by, our comfort level with each other increased significantly. For entertainment, Joshua and I went to movies, attended concerts, saw plays or walked the neighborhood. Josh seemed completely at ease with me even when we thought we might be spotted by the press. Had he been an elected official himself, I would have understood the anxiety; however, being the gay son of a highly respected local politician ought not to have been such a huge concern. Nobody wanted to be 'outed' least of all Joshua himself. I concluded that his fears were founded if he thought that his father would be discredited if it was revealed that his son was gay. How could anyone believe that having a gay offspring would lessen the credentials or value of an elected official or that of a parent?

In addition to being an elected official in the city of Gatineau, Josh's father owned a number of businesses in which all of the family members had been involved at one time or another. Andrew, Josh's colleague and close friend, was hired into the family businesses right out of college. In time, Joshua met all of Andrew's siblings including his four sisters. Monica, who worked for the Canadian Federal Government, had introduced Joshua to Henry knowing that their interest in music would lead to a lasting friendship. Had it not been for Henry, I doubt that Joshua would have come to my Christmas house party by himself.

Leesa, another of Andrew's sisters, was enamored with Josh and asked him to come to 'La Maison du citoyen' (Town Hall) to see her in a play that was written and produced by a local writer. She insisted that I attend as well. It was no surprise to me that at the intermission, I was introduced to Monica, Paula and Leesa, all curious to find out who I was. The crowd had gathered in the foyer while another function was happening on the second floor. Joshua looked up and to his surprise he spotted his parents. He had no idea that they would be there; he had been taken unawares.

Seconds later, Josh's parents were walking towards us. He greeted his mother first then his father, and rather than introducing me to his parents, he froze. Seeing his discomfort, his mother extended her hand and introduced herself to me. I was dazzled by her beauty and her incredible smile. She wanted to acknowledge me and say "hello" which she did in the most regal fashion. It hadn't taken her very long to figure out who I was standing next to her son, however Josh's Dad did not acknowledge my presence. They were gone in a flash; as they went back to the reception on the mezzanine level.

This first glimpse of Josh's parents told me a lot about him. He had inherited the charm, poise and grace of his mother; his good looks came from his parents. His father, a tall white-haired man with broad shoulders and contagious smile, was a magnet with women wherever he went. There was nothing ostentatious about them; they were simple folks with a lot of class. They had worked hard to amass considerable personal wealth and knew not to flaunt it.

When we got back to the apartment, I sensed that Joshua was beginning to calm down. We discussed what had happened in an open and honest way. I couldn't hide that I was somewhat disappointed in not being introduced to his father but I was not upset. This setback had the potential to disrupt our plans to live together. Joshua lived by the force and strength of his convictions and although they had wavered on that occasion, it was a sure bet that he could overcome his hesitancy.

As goes the expression 'when the going gets tough, the tough get going', Joshua turned to Henry for wise counsel. It was music that had brought them together. In difficult times,

Henry's words of wisdom were soothing and precisely what Josh needed to hear. They talked for hours. Invariably, it always came back to music. As avid collectors, Henry focused on all genres while Joshua collected disco, jazz and R&B. Their conversations typically included any news on the Disco front. The Queen of Disco, Donna Summer, as she was known in the 1970's, had recently been honored with her own 'star' on the Hollywood Walk of Fame. It was an accomplishment for the artist, a nod to disco music and an underlying statement about the power of the gay community's support for Donna Summer. Giorgio Moroder had done wonders with the Queen of Disco!

Talk of Québec's separation grew louder; we wondered how we would deal with this if it ever came to pass. Joshua was not about to give up his ties to the province of Québec and I had no desire to go back to live there permanently. When I made the move to Ontario in 1977, I was determined never to go back, although owning lakefront recreational property was not precluded. It wasn't a cultural issue that was holding me back, it was medical. To get good medical attention, many from the Québec side of the river came to Ottawa. That alone was enough to convince me that in the long run, I would be better living in Ontario where I would be able to access the best medical care in the country.

During periods of bad weather, we rented movies and stayed home. Curious to know what had caused Joshua to shed a few tears while watching 'Peggy Sue Got Married', we screened it one night and discussed its meaning. He explained that the movie brought flashbacks of his childhood; it reminded him of the unfulfilled dreams of his grandpa who had since passed away. His fondness for '60s and '70s music which is central to the soundtrack led to a lot of emotions as he watched the scenes unfold. A romantic at heart with a touch of nostalgia, Joshua was opening up to me at each step of the way. Nothing about him worried me; he was a decent, fun-loving, family guy who loved to play pranks. It was the child in him coming out in the most intriguing way. He considered himself an enigma and told me that I would continually be discovering new things about him every day. There would never be a dull moment.

On better days, we drove out of the city to visit the small towns, villages and hamlets in our search for 'Depression Glass' or that rare music record buried among worthless LPs in boxes stored in barns and antique shops along the way. One of our favorite stops was the Stittsville Flea Market on the outskirts of Ottawa, a twenty-minute drive from our downtown location. There were about half a dozen buildings each containing 30 to 40 vendors. On sunny warm days, another 100 to 125 outdoor vendors would arrive early on a Sunday morning to display their wares on makeshift showcases, tables or from the trunk of their cars. For the $1.50 parking fee, it amused us for a few hours. The earlier you got there, the better your chances of leaving with a rare find at a good price, particularly if you had been lucky enough to buy it from one of the good-weather vendors who worked outside.

The conversation about living together continued all the while. Joshua agreed that my apartment could become 'our' apartment if he could bring some of his stuff. We talked about turning the second bedroom into a den where Josh's music collection could be stored. There was a suggestion that it might be wise for us to find a new place, one that we would agree to, but that in the interim, the 250 O'Connor apartment would do fine. I was in no hurry to leave what I considered to be an exceptional building. As rent controls had limited the yearly increases, our monthly costs were below market average; going elsewhere would likely mean paying a lot more for similar accommodations.

17

My First Love, Jean

A new chapter of my life began when I met Jean Bélair at Sacs, a popular Hull discothèque. Norman had insisted that I join him at this fashionable dance venue for an evening of good music and people watching. Disco fever was at its highest point in April 1978. As the evening progressed, the volume increased making it tempting to join the throng of beautiful men on the dance floor. My body was swaying to the music when an older but very attractive man asked me to dance. No words were spoken; he simply held his hand out and pointed towards the dance floor. I followed him to the centre of the crowd as if to hide from prying eyes. We danced nonstop for nearly twenty minutes; the disc jockey had cleverly strung the music in a non-ending medley without any clear break that would have made it easy to say 'thank you' and walk off the floor. When I signaled that I needed a break, we walked to the back of the club where we were able to hear each other as we introduced ourselves and exchanged pleasantries.

Unbeknownst to me at the time, Sacs had quite a reputation: in part due to the fact that one of the members of the Village People had been there after a Sunday evening performance in Ottawa. Dressed in full costume, he entered the club on 'Rue du Portage' and greeted his many fans who were stunned to see him without a full escort. He sat down at a table that had been reserved for him.

'I hear that this place was so trendy that heterosexuals wanted in,' said Josh.

'You're right,' I said. 'At times, it was difficult to know if the person you were looking at was gay or straight. If a man didn't look at you, you still weren't sure whether or not it was a lack of interest or that he was looking for a woman. To add to the confusion some guys were cruising other guys, and later showing an interest in women.'

'Was Jean playing both sides of the fence?' asked Josh.

'No, I didn't think so.' I said. 'That night, he definitely wanted to know more about me.'

'What did you find out about him that first night?' said Josh.

Sacs wasn't a very large club and to get away from the noise, you really had to move to the outer walls as far away from the gigantic speakers as you could and even there, it was difficult to have a conversation. I was expecting him to ask the most often-used line by people who met in bars at the time, 'do you come here often?' If you answered 'yes', you came across as being somewhat easy; if you answered 'no', chances are the other person would ask you, 'where do you go when you go out?' I was astonished when Jean avoided the crass small talk and went straight to the point by introducing himself. Finally, someone with class, I thought to myself.

Jean didn't reveal his age but I could tell that he was older than me; how much older, I couldn't really guess and I really didn't care. About the same height as me, he was well dressed in a conservative but classic style. His graying hair was well groomed and everything about him was clean cut. Weighing approximately 145 pounds, his 5 feet 8 inch body was well proportioned. One distinguishing feature were the marks left by the ravages of acne suffered years ago. He did his best to hide them; it didn't take away from his better-than-average facial features. Even before we had spoken to each other, I had the impression that he was an intelligent man. My hunch proved accurate.

We left the bar together that night and headed for his apartment in an upscale area of the city, one that I had as yet to discover. Upon entering his home, my jaw dropped; he noticed the look of surprise on my face and admitted that he was an interior designer working for the Federal Government. It quickly dawned on me that Jean was the person I had always wanted to be. I had hoped to become an interior designer, to be well established and to live in an up-scale pad. Jean had it all; he traveled the world working on the redesign of embassies and chancelleries in far away places the names of which were very foreign to me at the time. I often confused Jeddah and Jakarta yet they are thousands of miles apart.

When Jean was away, which was often, I went to his apartment to water the plants and admire the stunning interiors he had created. Days before he was due back in Ottawa, I would clean his place so that we could spend more time together. Before he set foot in his kitchen, I had stocked the refrigerator with the necessities thus saving him from having to step out and pick up items we would need to make breakfast the following morning.

There was always a gift for me hidden in Jean's luggage; he diligently bought hand-made souvenirs from the countries he visited. On most trips, he added to his owl collection which was tastefully displayed in all of the rooms of his cozy two-bedroom apartment. Twelve years my senior, Jean was much wiser than I and his owl collection served as a permanent reminder that we were not on a level playing field. The age difference did not seem to bother him and at first, I did not mind it although I could sense that some of his friends thought that he had robbed the cradle.

'Are you interested in joining us in Provincetown in the fall?' asked Jean.

'Where is Provincetown and who will be there?' I replied.

'Provincetown is an old Portuguese fishing village at the tip of Cape Cod; it emerged as a meeting place for homosexuals after the Second World War. As gay men wanted to get away from the limelight, this idyllic out-of-the-way village with its sandy dunes became the perfect place to congregate. In the past thirty years, it has grown exponentially and is now one of America's top gay resorts. My friends and I meet there every year for Labor Day. Some stay for 3 to 4 days while others spend the week as the shoulder season begins after the crowds leave on the Monday of the long weekend.'

'What about accommodations?' I asked.

'All of us Canadians rent out all of Tillie's units on Bradford Street,' said Jean. 'It's not very fancy but the location is perfect and the price is right. She rents out two units next to her house and four across the street adjacent to her husband's wrought iron workshop. Each unit has a full kitchen and bathroom; most meals are taken outside on the patio and shared with the gang.'

'How long will it take us to get there?' I enquired.

'I like to leave in the wee hours of the morning so that we can get to Hyannis before late afternoon,' said Jean. 'It's much cheaper to buy food there than in P-town.'

'P-town?' I repeated Jean's last words.

'Yes, that's how most people refer to Provincetown,' Jean replied. 'You'll really like this place. It's laid back; everybody is there for a good time. There are plenty of restaurants, interesting art galleries and stores to say nothing about the hunks that roam the streets and the dunes. Every day, we pack up for a day at the beach and come back to the room in time to wash up and get dressed to go to the tea-dance at the Boatslip.'

'They serve tea at the Boatslip?' I said.

'Not quite,' said Jean with a broad smile. 'A tea-dance is just a name for a late afternoon party where beer and cocktails are served and where people boogie on the dance floor. They mingle around the pool area which is very entertaining to watch.'

In the weeks leading up to the trip to P-town, Jean helped me decide what to pack. What would I wear at a tea-dance? Brightly colored polo shirts were the rage; I would wear off-white shorts and horizontally striped polo shirts. My fear was that I would stick out like a sore thumb; I wanted to blend in so that people would not pay much attention to me. When we finally got there and I saw the beautiful men with toned and tanned bodies, I knew I did not need to worry that anyone would be staring at me. There were so many interesting and good-looking men that I would certainly go unnoticed.

Visiting P-town at the height of tourist season is like being in a candy store. The variety of people was amazing: all ages, all body types, all colors, all nationalities and all dressed to the "nines".

Race Point Beach was the place to be from 10 am onwards. There, couples and groups gathered around blankets and beach towels laid in a quilt-like pattern. For every two or three, there was a cooler filled with wine, beer, and food. Some guys read books while others played Frisbee or swam in Cape Cod Bay. Listed as one of the best in the United States, Race Point Beach catered to a diverse crowd. Those who got there by car usually stayed within 500 meters of the parking lot. The lesbian crowd usually went a bit further down the beach creating their own space. Gay men went to the end of the beach, the nudist area. Not all were naked; many paraded around in sexy swimwear. It was almost like attending a fashion show to see the guys strut up and down the length of the beach, and stopping here and there to chat with friends or people they had recently met at the bars in town, or slept with the night before!

At about 3 pm, sun-seekers began to get ready for the walk back to town through the sand dunes. Some would stop in the bushes on the way back. Sex in public was tolerated so long as the men made sure that they could not been seen.

Back in town, it was time to get ready for cocktails at the Boatslip. The hot water gauge of all hotels and inns must certainly have been at the highest point between 4 and 5 pm as the crowd got cleaned up in time for tea-dance. Walking down Commercial Street from both directions, men of all types were heading for P-town's most important social event of the day at the Boatslip. Dressed in their finest and sexiest outfits, they offered quite the parade to those sitting in deck chairs in front of the many establishments along the main drag (pardon the pun!).

Commercial Street, the main throughway of P-town runs East-West. The village has two parallel streets: Commercial and Bradford. Restaurants, bars, galleries, stores, hotels, inns, and B&Bs line these streets from the west end at the tip of the peninsula to the east end nearing North Truro. Once tea-dance was over, 500 to 600 men sashayed down the streets. It was chow time and never difficult to find a good restaurant as there was always a new one opening to great fanfare.

All but a few businesses stayed open late every night. A postprandial stroll was a must to see and be seen in. We walked into every antique and curio shop to check out new stock. Numerous art galleries offered such a mesmerizing array of art that it was difficult to leave without making a purchase. Book stores and clothing stores, although fewer, carried items sure to appeal to gay men. If money had been no object, I could have spent a fortune every day.

By the end of the week, the party was over. It was time to get back to reality. I was starting my second year of teaching at

Gatineau Elementary. I looked forward to seeing those fresh new faces.

Time was moving on and things were changing. As a sign of the times, the production of the Volkswagen Beetle had stopped after almost 30 years and 20 million vehicles produced. The Beetle had been the ubiquitous vehicle of my time, one that I had wanted to own. Built for the common folk, it was affordable and cheap to operate, a vehicle that someday I would want to buy by never did. For me, it meant the end of a major symbol of that period but life went on. Having Jean around made life bearable. I was thankful for the pillar of support he was to me although I would not have admitted it at the time.

Back in his apartment on Rideau Terrace, we spent many evenings in front of the fireplace listening to Jane Oliver. Her soothing voice was the perfect antidote to the horrors the world was witnessing at the time. Cult leader Jim Jones had instructed over 900 members of his church, "People's Temple", to commit suicide in Guyana. Had the world gone mad? We comforted each other; our relationship gave us what we needed to carry on in the face of world events that seemed to go from sad to disastrous.

18

Two Marriages and a Death

In those early days of our relationship, Joshua and I entertained as often as we could. It was a good way to meet each other's friends. One of our first dinner parties was organized so that I would meet Louisa, his sister, and her fiancé Sergio. We carefully planned the meal and the theme. Spring was just around the corner. It inspired us to put together an arrangement of daffodils which sat on a black table cloth with yellow napkins and yellow candles. Stunning, I thought to myself. We settled on 'Osso Bucco' as the main course even though I was making this recipe for the first time. It would have been easier to cook a time-tested recipe rather than trying something new especially when having people over for the first time. Undaunted by the enormity of the task, my objective was to make a very good first impression suspecting that the details of the evening would be relayed to Josh's parents. Joshua guided me as he had seen his mother put it together many times before. Asparagus wrapped in smoked salmon for the appetizer and cheese cake for dessert met with Josh's approval. To my surprise, Louisa's favorite food was smoked salmon. I was anxious that the meat would be tough or the sauce too spicy; needless to say, it was a huge success and not one ounce of it was left over

Like mother, like daughter, I thought to myself. Louisa was very much like her mother in many ways; everything was just perfect including hair, makeup and clothing. Wearing a navy cocktail dress with a string of pearls, her smile revealing beautiful white teeth said it all. She was in full control of herself; she exuded a confidence demonstrated through well-articulated statements on all of the topics we covered that evening. Sergio, on the other hand, was not as comfortable with us and certainly not as refined as his wife-to-be. A strikingly tall good-looking young man with salt-and-pepper hair and a dreadful set of teeth, he had less formal education than Louisa; the school of life had taught him most of what he knew. With wedding plans well underway, they shared with us some of the details of the event that was scheduled for early June.

I was definitely not invited to this wedding; Joshua had been given the ungrateful task of informing me. He felt divided; he wanted to be loyal to his family but felt that leaving me behind was wrong. At first, the thought of being excluded annoyed me. Thinking it through, I realized that even if the circumstances had been entirely different, my presence would raise all kinds of questions. Who is this person? Why is Joshua accompanied by an older guy? Josh's relatives did not know about me; it would have been inappropriate for me to be introduced then when the focus was on the newlyweds. Letting go, I came to the conclusion that there would be a more opportune time to make my entry into Josh's family, and the timing of such an occasion would likely be outside of my control.

'Does it upset you not to be invited to my sister's wedding?' asked Joshua.

'Quite frankly, I'm rather relieved,' I replied. 'I really don't think that we should be imposing ourselves on your family. When the time is right, we will get an invitation for a meal or an event. Eventually, either your mother or your sister will be so anxious to meet me that they will want to include me in a family event. My guess is that your sister will do it first.'

'Will you feel comfortable in their presence?' he enquired.

'From all the information you have given me on your family, I would be very surprised if things didn't go well. They all seem very gracious and respectful; absent a major faux pas, I should be able to handle myself in a manner that will earn respect from all of them,' I answered confidently. 'All I hope is that the conversation does not turn to sports or other topics of which I know very little.'

'Not to worry, my mother and sister will do most of the talking; you'll have a hard time getting a word in edgewise!' he said half-jokingly.

'When that day comes, I'll have you brief me on each person I'm going to meet and on the proper way of addressing them.

Family etiquette varies and I do not want to mess up on the very first visit I have with them. Gosh, I'm getting nervous just talking about it. Can we change the subject?'

Another wedding, planned for November, got me excited. My youngest brother Danny was finally tying the knot. Marianne, his bride-to-be, was a lovely woman whose grace and maturity had been inherited from her own mother, a woman whose style, poise and intellect impressed anyone who met her. I was thrilled that my kid brother was marrying into a family whose values were similar to ours. In my opinion, their chances of success were very high. With luck, Geoffrey would still be healthy enough to attend.

So many of my friends were unwell. It was a sad time, one that lasted for years, unfortunately. Gerry and Richard kept us informed of everyone's progress; Darryl Benoit was getting quite weak, Roger Bell was frail and Reggie Altman and his partner Ian Smith were in remission. HIV and AIDS were still ravaging my circle of friends. The group was getting smaller with every passing week. I tried not to focus on the loss of my dear friends but rather on the love that Joshua and I shared. I often wondered if I would be next in line for death row; yet I was not sick, nor did I have any reason to worry. Medical advances made it possible to extend one's life, but was it worth it? Who would want to live longer when the quality of such a life was so poor?

One day I was up, the next I was down. The emotional rollercoaster was on-going. Josh's love made me high as a kite; the pain and the distress my friends were going through quickly brought me down and made me feel so sad. I felt helpless, totally useless. When I spent time with any one of my dear ill friends, words would not come to me. Choking back the tears, I would do my best to hide my feelings by putting on a smile that must have looked rather artificial. How could all of this be happening so early in my life? Was this retribution for a life of sin? Were the bible-belters right in their assessment of gays? Surely a loving God would help us find a way out of this mess, a way of handling the pain, the loss and the suffering. I was not well equipped for dealing with this sort of catastrophe and my faith in God was being tested to the limits.

Death was all around me. Barbara Frum's passing at the age of 54 following an eighteen-year battle with leukemia left me numb. This Canadian radio and television journalist had pioneered a tough interview style that brought her much success in her years with the Canadian Broadcasting Corporation. My mother had also been a huge fan; she would have been saddened by this tragic loss of life. Because of my mother, I had started listening to Barbara Frum; her demise just added to the mountain of sorrow I was carrying at the time.

Nothing moves one to want to live more than the fear of dying. Not that I had a death wish, but there were days I wondered why I was being spared. Those who were getting ready for the afterlife were, in a way, avoiding the eventual process of aging, something most gay men fear from a very young age. What is considered old changes as one gets older. In my twenties, anyone over 40 was ancient. What could these shriveled up people do at that age? Having just turned 40 a few months ago, I now knew that age is just a number; I felt no differently than I had 20 years previously.

Still, life and death issues were part of the discussion most days. During the sex-crazed years of the '70s, I was no saint. While I did not indulge in risky sexual behaviors, I certainly had my fair share of partners, any one of whom could have been an HIV carrier. Not everyone wanted to be tested lest one finds out he is HIV positive. Usually, a person waited for symptoms to show up before deciding to get tested. Anonymous testing had become the norm; gay men were encouraged to get themselves checked. I resisted the call for two reasons; I knew I wouldn't be able to deal with a positive diagnosis. The friends who would have been able to help me were either very ill or had already passed away. Another reason was that I felt I had been wise by abstaining from most of the sexual practices that were considered to be high risk. Foolishly, I was determined to avoid confronting a verdict.

It was just a matter of time before Joshua and I would have a discussion on this very topic. Planning for the long term, he wanted to know where I stood with him. He felt that it would be wise for us to know my HIV status so that we could take appropriate precautions, if need be. He had tested HIV negative not long before I met him and although he wasn't pushing me to follow suit, he certainly made it clear that it would be expected that I get tested.

This could have been a show stopper potentially ending our relationship. That was too great a risk for me. There had been a momentum building in our relationship, but this certainly could put the brakes on. The choice was mine. His mother had been heard saying that she would not be upset if he moved out. It was assumed that he was moving in with me. Would I risk this once-in-a-lifetime opportunity to live with the man I loved just out of fear of an HIV test?

19

Walking a Tightrope

Life had taken a turn towards normalcy in 1978. Each day, I drove to Gatineau where I taught French as a second language to boys and girls ranging in age from 5 to 8. It quickly became routine. The kids were the reason I stayed in that job as long as I did. Aside from a few difficult children, the students were adorable. It was hard not to have favorites and I did my best to hide my preferences. Ray, a handsome boy with above-average intelligence had stolen my heart. Had there been a need, I would have adopted him in a flash even with the fear of accusations of pedophilia that could have been made against me. I would not have thought twice about making such a huge commitment, he was that special. Although I had said publicly that I did not want to have children, I could not have imagined seeing this young boy without a parent.

The Ministry of Education of the Province of Québec had hired teaching assistants so that French could be taught to smaller groups. While I conducted French lessons to half a class, my assistant took the other half and kept them busy doing social activities, *en français*! In a day, I taught eight groups of approximately twelve students. By the end of the day, I was exhausted. When the final bell rang at 3:20, I was out the door at the same time as the hordes of young screaming kids running towards their school buses or their parents waiting at the school gate.

My relationship with Jean had also become routine. We saw each other once during the week and, on weekends, I moved in with him. Hardly a week went by that we didn't have a party to attend. It seemed to me that Jean was friendly with half the world. He enjoyed meeting new people and struck up conversations very easily. The world revolved around him; I felt like Toto from the Wizard of Oz. Habitually, I was the youngest in a crowd. Since I did not always feel that I belonged, it created tensions in our relationship.

I remember one such party in Montréal in September; Tim Lawlor was turning 40. His partner, Tim Abbott, had arranged an open house with the landlords (Michel and Guy) who lived on the lower level of an upscale Côtes des Neiges two-story stone house. Most of the people attending were much older than I and most were coupled. Party goers filled both levels of the house going from one area to another. Food was plentiful and exquisitely arranged on large platters; liquor and wine flowed. Tim was showered with gifts, mostly books or flowers. Jean was having a great time rekindling friendships with people he didn't get to see very often.

To pass the time away, I analyzed every detail of the decorating scheme in each of the rooms. My memory of the living room décor remains vivid. A highly floral fabric, generously pleated, had been used to cover the walls. A huge crystal chandelier hung dead center from the ceiling; angled fabric from this point joined the four walls and created a virtual tent. The effect was stunning albeit a tad feminine to my liking. Never again would I see such a dramatic decorating effect done with fabric. Michel and Guy were proud of this unique style that reflected their taste in modern interiors. Moving from one room to another, I spoke to a few people who wondered with whom I had come to this glorious event. It was late before Jean decided to leave the festivities and drive back to Ottawa. My boredom hadn't gone unnoticed; we had a difficult conversation in which I expressed my uneasiness with having to befriend older people with whom I had little in common.

There were days that I felt that I was walking a fine line not unlike the acrobat Karl Wallenda whose death after falling off a tightrope resonated with me. I knew Jean was extremely proud of me and enjoyed introducing me to his many friends and acquaintances. While I kept my feelings to myself most of time, the truth came out at awkward moments. I knew it hurt him; I felt bad for revealing my deepest thoughts. Many of my friends considered me very fortunate to have such a generous partner; they would gladly have changed places with me. As much as I admired him and was comfortable in his surroundings, I came to the realization we were drifting apart. Was I throwing away the baby with the bathwater? What was wrong with me? Although our relationship had been a monogamous one, I didn't feel committed.

Thanks to Frenchy who shared the same birthday with Jean and with whom she had built a comfortable friendship, she got his perspective on our relationship. He had confided in her when all hell broke loose the day I told him that I needed space. Norman came to my rescue offering wise counsel. He had just split with Marcello; the pain of separation was fresh in his mind. He and I spent hours analyzing every detail of my liaison with Jean. We came to the same conclusion: neither of us was to blame. We were not meant for each other. Or had not met at the right time.

A couple of months passed during which we kept our distance. The longer I waited to make a decision, the harder it got. Agonizingly, I decided I would give it another try hoping that this time we would avoid the difficulties that had led to our first separation, yet I couldn't put a finger on what exactly was the issue. Was it lack of passion? Frenchy cheered us on; she loved us very dearly and wanted us to be together. Would our second attempt last any longer that the 33 days of Pope Jean Paul I?

My fondest memories of Jean are the times we spent watching sitcoms laying on his bed. "Three's Company" was one of our favorites. Mr. Roper's wink at the camera seemed like an acknowledgement that not all needs to be said and one can share deep thoughts with a kindred spirit without verbalizing.

20

Death and the Afterlife

AIDS had become epidemic; the acronym was on everybody's lips. It was no longer an illness limited to gay men; it had spread to other communities. There was no ignoring it brought unwanted attention to the gay community. At first a big city disease, by now people from every corner of the planet were being affected by this dreadful disease. Bible thumpers believed that it was God's revenge for a sick and depraved part of society they so wanted to get rid of desperately. Slowly the world was waking up to what was initially feared to be a pandemic. With the eventual discovery of pharmaceutical drugs prolonging the life of AIDS patients, a limited number of end-of-life hospices began to sprout. The caring of the sick and dying brought the gay community together to temporarily stop the in-fighting. Heart wrenching as it was, life went on.

The day had come for me to be tested for HIV. The test is not the issue; it's the verdict. Every day, someone in my circle of friends was diagnosed HIV positive; would I be the next in line? I couldn't help but wonder if Joshua would stick around if it came to that. Would a perfectly healthy, young and attractive guy want to share his life with a sick old man? I had my doubts!

It wasn't so much the fear of dying, although most people would feel apprehensive about passing, but the stigma and the pain of illness that haunted me. In the early days of the AIDS epidemic, we spoke in hushed tones when discussing this dreaded disease or the condition of any of our friends who were suffering from the endless infections caught as a result of an immune system incapable of fighting off opportunistic viruses. The fear of losing one friend after the other led to bouts of anxiety and depression. In comparison to what others were going through, I resolved to find the ways and means to retain a sense of well-being despite the sense of doom and gloom that prevailed in those days. Even with some early breakthroughs in research labs, there was very little optimism amongst my circle of friends. Would I be the sole survivor of the group or would I also succumb to this horrific illness? Some days, I avoided all contact with people who were ill, all newspapers and magazines and stayed away from anything that reminded me, or that brought me back to the subject of AIDS. It was my coping method, one that worked for me, but was never discussed with others for fear of repudiation.

During a conversation at a party to celebrate Simon's 40th birthday, Luke informed me that Neil was going fast; he was now at death's door. He mentioned in passing that Guillaume had died a year ago and that he hadn't seen his spouse, Shamus, since the funeral. This was a strange conversation with a person who looked like he was about to die himself. At 5 feet 8 inches, Luke was a thin man with no body fat whatsoever. He had been skin and bones since the first day I met him. Any disease would strike him down in a flash; I think he knew this.

It was arthritis and not AIDS that was at my heels. Dr. Zable gave me the depressing news; contact lenses were out of the question.

Uveitis — a form of arthritis — had permanently damaged my right eye; wearing contacts would cause needless irritation. A short discussion on glaucoma was enough for me to agree with his recommendation that I wear glasses.

A break from the constant doom and gloom took the form of an invitation to attend Mike and Halley's wedding. I was thrilled that we were being invited as a couple. Joshua and Mike had been buddies for years; they had studied at the same university and shared many common friends. For me, this was an acknowledgement of our relationship; Mike and Halley had been supportive of us although they knew very little about me other than what Joshua had told them. This vote of confidence was a welcome relief from the heaviness of the cycle of death that had been circling around us for years.

William Street Wine Bar was the place to be and be seen on a Sunday afternoon. I looked forward to late afternoon outings; it had become a replacement for the late night bar scene that had long ago lost its appeal. Now partnered, the attraction to bars and clubs had vanished. This wine bar was the perfect place to meet and chat with friends. The background music was never too loud. The art-nouveau color scheme of black, grey and peach gave the place an air of sophistication.

Just as I came in, I spotted Lawrence sitting at the bar. He was a popular person; there were always many other guys around him. When he saw me, he came towards me to chat. After customary greetings, the conversation shifted to the health of our friends. Donald Romaine was ill; according to Lawrence, Donald had Hodgkin's disease but the word on the street was that Donald was hiding the fact that he was HIV positive. A man of means, Donald was as private as he was exuberant; he was a flamboyant type but not effeminate in any way. He was known to host exotic parties; an invitation to one of his many wild evenings was a mark of trust. We knew each other as we sang in the Ottawa Men's Chorus; there, he would try to impress others with his lavish lifestyle. I was never part of his close-knit circle of friends and information I had of those nights in the dungeon were third-party tidbits.

More news came concerning Neil whose eyesight had gone and so was now wishing to die. Darryl Benoit was nearing the end. There was so much sad news that it was difficult to be positive. Having Joshua around helped me through the difficult moments. Most of my friends were either ill or dying; Joshua did not know them very well as I did not spend much time with them. I blame myself for not being up to visiting bedridden friends; the mere thought of it made me feel uncomfortable. Rather than being in their presence and feeling out of place, I stayed away out of respect for their privacy.

Distractions were few; Joshua and I watched the official opening of Euro Disney on television. It was a dazzling spectacle that included top-notch performers from around the world. Joshua had been to Disney World in Florida and enjoyed the magic created by this extraordinary team of designers.

The fantasy created by Walt Disney was in sharp contrast with the pain and suffering of the gay community around the world. Despite it all, for every person who had died of AIDS, a quilt was made (by friends and family of the deceased) and added to the international quilt started in the United States. Each panel told the story of a person whose life had been cut short. As colorful as any Disney creation, it was a memorial that touched the millions who came to see it in the various towns and cities in North America.

The death of Neil Davidson and Tony Kingston within days of each other was a hard blow.

'Do you believe in past lives?' enquired Josh. 'That unfinished business in one life is carried over to the next?'

'Funny that you talk about reincarnation,' I said. 'Aunt Annie and I had long debates about this. She was convinced that when the soul leaves the body, it eventually comes back to earth in another being to further the work of improving oneself or to find redemption for past wrongful deeds.'

'What do you think of a person who has tremendous talent but without having had to acquire it?' said Josh.

'Are you referring to child prodigies?' I asked.

'Yes! That's exactly what I mean,' said Josh. 'I think these people had a talent in a former life and continue where they left off in a previous incarnation. How else could you explain how a young child can play Beethoven with all the energy and inspiration his compositions require?'

'Conversely, a person may go through life paying dearly for mistakes from previous lives,' I said. 'At least, that's the way I see it. *Not fair* you might think, but I believe that we are here to learn, and unless we do, we are committed to relive the same mistakes over and over until we understand what it is that we should learn.'

'I've read that family members were sometimes related to each other in previous lives; your mother may have been your sister or your daughter in an earlier life,' said Josh. 'That can explain some of the rivalries between siblings who may have hated or despised each other in a prior existence.'

'Would past life regression be helpful in finding former relationships?' Joshua wondered. 'We should rent the movie, Dead Again. This 1991 film details the 1949 murder of pianist known as Margaret who was stabbed with a pair of antique scissors during a robbery. Her husband, Roman, is found guilty of the crime and sentenced to death. The plot is very twisted; in the end we learn that Roman was not guilty of the crime. Much of what is learned about the murder comes through past-life regression sessions.'

Strong chemistry between Joshua and I got me thinking about whether or not we had been connected in any way in a previous life. At times, I thought he was clairvoyant; he was able to read my thoughts with an uncanny and unnerving precision. I suspected he had supernatural gifts; he made light of the fact that he was indeed quite capable of premonition and had strong visionary dreams. He chose not to speak about these abilities probably for fear of my reactions. He need not have worried. The more I knew about Josh, the more I wanted to continue on our journey of discovery.

Through the written works of Edgar Cayce, I had learned much about the spiritual world and Cayce's powers of healing. He performed oftentimes off location (in some cases, hundreds of miles away from the person he was treating), directing the attending physician to perform delicate operations that led to unbelievable recoveries from an illness where few people rarely survived. Past-life regressions allowed Cayce to pinpoint the source of problems and to establish suitable remedies which were unconventional. Joshua took a keen interest in these writings. We came to realize that we both believed in karmic law, and that whatever good we can do on earth is not lost at death. Believing in purpose and natural justice is the strongest foundation we can expect to have. We felt destined for each other; Joshua sensed that our time together would cover many decades, perhaps a lifetime.

21

Switching Gears

It was a hot night in July 1980 in Ottawa and the air in my small Chapel Street apartment was stifling. A small fan in the hallway right in front of a window and just across the main entrance could not cool down the trailer-like apartment where one room led into the next all along the length of the tenement building. With a southern exposure for all windows, with the exception of the one in the bedroom which faced east, my abode was a furnace during the summer months. Fortunately, there was a veranda I could use when the heat got to me. This open space was the entry point to several other units in the building; it was also my perch to watch the passers-by going to the Laundromat across the street on Somerset.

I was sitting on the front steps sipping a soda and watching the world go by when I saw Michael walking up the street in my direction. I had known him for some time; we had been introduced at a private party I cannot recall. Michael's toned body wrapped in expensive clothing said much about him. By all accounts, he took good care of himself. It was reasonable to conclude that he was healthy and not probably affected by HIV.

When he got close to where I was sitting, he stopped to chat. Pleasantries aside, he told me that he was dating my former partner. Would I mind? Hell no! Jean and I had given it a good try; there was no sense in prolonging a relationship that wasn't working for either of us. Our inevitable break-up had been harder on me the second time, as it was Jean who had dealt the final blow. There was no acrimony between us; we knew we had come full circle and it was time to get off the merry-go-round.

I felt relieved that Jean had met Michael; they had much in common and would likely have a long and fulfilling liaison. They liked the arts, high-end clothing, and interior design as well as gourmet foods. It helped that Michael was an excellent chef having learned a lot from his mother. Curious to hear my side of the story, he wanted to know why Jean and I had gone our separate ways. Never one to hide behind walls, I shared with him the things that had initially attracted me to Jean and the issues that tore us apart. From the short time he had been with him, he had already picked up on a few irritants that had him worried. I encouraged him to iron out their differences so that their relationship could develop into a long-term bond, the kind I would have wanted with Jean.

After the break-up with Jean, my personal life was a bit shaky and my professional life was no better. Unsure that I wished to remain a school teacher, the thought of having to redirect my life once again made me fearful of what lay ahead. Principal Warden called me into his office and said that he felt I was not cut out to be an elementary school teacher; I wasn't showing the passion it takes to spend a career teaching young kids. According to Hank, *the money is good but after a while it will be impossible for you to get out.* I knew what he meant; so many teachers had stayed because of the salary and not for the sake of the children. Mr. Warden's words echoed in my mind every day at the end of every grueling day.

Dreams of becoming an interior designer had vanished when I failed to get enough credits at the end of my first year of university. I had turned to teaching as a stepping stone to another undefined career. Not knowing where I would eventually find suitable employment, I decided that, if things went poorly, I could always make a few dollars supply teaching in local schools. The path to success was very foggy; I really didn't have a clue about where or what I should be doing next. I needed time to think, to find myself, to reinvent myself. I was buying time. So scared was I that I would be a failure, I made a decision to go back to university for a one-year Bachelor of Education degree. As counterproductive as it appeared, my reasoning was that having a degree in education and a few years of experience would ensure an income if worse came to worse. It would become my back-up plan just in case my life journey led me to a dead-end. Abort and reboot!

Going back to university gave me the jitters; I would likely be the oldest of my cohort. On the positive side, my experience would come in handy. Educational theory would either make sense to me or be so off the wall that it could be laughable. This was going to be a walk in the park or at least that's what I believed when I registered at the Lamoureux Pavilion at Ottawa University.

The class of 1981 was divided into two groups; I belonged to the smaller subgroup who were destined to become elementary school teachers. There weren't many men but of the ones that were in my class, Luc was my favorite. He had worked as a graphic designer for a number of years and had felt the calling to become a teacher. Like a religious calling, a person can feel the pull which in his case was difficult to ignore. Luc was an outdoorsman; he liked hiking, biking, snowshoeing, skiing and most other non-team sporting activities. Married with three children, his girls were the highlight of his life. His elegant wife, Christine, a beautiful tall and blonde-haired woman with a granola bent, was already an elementary school teacher.

My attraction to Luc grew from the first day I met him. He was by far the most attractive guy in our group. Try as I might to hide my feelings, my fellow students had figured out that I had a mad crush on him. It was all for naught as he was happily married and very 'straight'. When he came to early morning classes with bags under his eyes, he would smile at me and say, *I was attacked late last night.* One day, I retorted by saying that pillows don't attack. He knew I lived alone; I told him I was gay. Fortunately, that didn't scare him; he continued the friendship as though that had no bearing at all. He felt comfortable enough to invite me to meet his wife and children. In the years that followed, we saw each other only a few times; I did not pursue teaching and therefore would not have had the opportunity to bump into him at meetings or professional development days.

22

Good News

In the days leading up to the 1992 Easter long weekend, Joshua arranged to spend time with me knowing that we would not be seeing each other on Easter Sunday. Family came first. His parents were young and enjoyed having their children with them at all the special events of the year. There would be many more weekends and holidays without him; I would have to get used to it. To compensate for this absence, Joshua planned a few outdoor activities on the Friday and Saturday preceding Easter. A stroll in the Byward Market in the spring was my idea of a good time. Pussy willows, maple syrup and daffodils were displayed at every corner; there was an air of optimism that better and warmer times were ahead. With winter behind us and daylight extending a bit more every 24 hours, my spirits improved with each passing day.

I noticed that Joshua also felt very upbeat; was he also a fan of spring? Yes! We agreed that the start of the growth cycle was the beginning of a new year full of hopefulness, and clean venues without the accumulated debris made by tourists and others who litter our pristine environment. People in the service industry were much jollier at the launch of the tourist season than they would be in the fall when aching bones and short tempers would be the norm.

We further discussed our living together. The 1200 square foot apartment was a good size but I had filled it up in the seven years that I had occupied it before meeting Josh. Of the two bedrooms, the smaller one became my master bedroom. Josh's belongings, including his music collection could fit into the larger bedroom. Our plan was to turn that room into a den complete with television and cabinets to store books, CDs, LPs, etcetera.

We were worried that the weight of all the stuff in the room would impact on the wood structure of the building but a steel beam the length of the building, which could be seen in the basement, led us to believe that the floors would be able to handle the extra load. It would take years before we would notice a one-inch separation between the baseboard and the floor, indicating that the excess burden had created a problem.

Our plan was to live in that apartment as long as we could while looking for a more suitable place. Ideally, our next home would be a bit larger to accommodate all of our worldly possessions. We each wanted a computer desk and easy access to our resource materials. This was paramount for Josh; he had begun doing research on the 'disco' period with the hope of producing some sort of anthology, the parameters of which were still very sketchy.

Surprising news came my way in early May 1992. I couldn't believe my ears when I was told that I was HIV negative. *Are you sure?* None of my friends were surprised; the opposite would have been a shocker. Granted, I hadn't indulged in risky sexual behaviors; I knew back then about protecting myself: I knew where I had been. In the past 25 years, I had had my fair share of encounters some of which I would never talk about.

I had come to the conclusion that I was HIV positive without any symptoms and without testing. There was no need to be concerned, or so I thought. It did matter to me that Joshua needed to know for sure. Not having obvious symptoms wasn't enough for him; he needed a medical confirmation with regards to my HIV status. If I expected to keep him around, I had no choice but to be tested. This good news came as a big surprise to me, and as relief to Josh. We were now ready to move forward, confident that any other potential roadblock to our plans for moving in together would be insignificant in comparison.

The test results gave me a feeling of euphoria; it meant a new lease on life, a second chance, a get-out-of-jail-free. It was like winning a lottery — the lotto of life. I made sure I was alone when I got the news out of fear for what I suspected. Alleluia! My life would go on.

Whether he realized it or not, Joshua had been holding back on me. I felt he was putting the brakes on our relationship without so much as admitting to it. It was only natural that he should protect himself and his family. He always took into consideration the potential impacts on his immediate family.

On the job front, things were happening. A half-day assessment for a Staffing Consultant position at the Public Service Commission had left me feeling good about winning one of the four vacancies that had been advertised. Although it wouldn't amount to a promotion in terms of salary, it was definitely the type of job I had wanted for some time. I had joined the human resources team in 1986 and worked in various capacities. Staffing had been my passion and through a number of assignments, I had gained considerable experience in both line and central agency organizations. To ensure broad experience which would be needed to move up the ladder, I had agreed to work in a regional office for a period of ten months. As a staffing specialist, I felt I had a good grasp of the subject matter so when the Staffing Consultancy positions opened up, I knew I was ready for the challenge.

Of all the qualities Joshua displayed, it was his sense of humor that I found so endearing. Even in the strangest of situations, he could find the funny side of things. His laughter was loud and from the heart. Every week, we would get our humor fix by watching a sitcom. One of our all time favorites was The Golden Girls. We were sad on the day that we watched the final episode. After seven seasons, we had become attached to Dorothy, Rose, Blanche and Sofia. It was the funny lines, the zingers, the corny jokes and the comical situations that the girls faced in each episode that made us crack up. Humour was one of the cornerstones of our relationship. In a time when we were attending two to three memorials a month, the lighter side of life kept us going. Just as Dorothy threatened her mother by mentioning the Shady Pines senior's home when she was being a pain, we kidded each other by suggesting that he would move back home when the going got rough. It was all in jest; we were so happy together that the thought of Joshua not coming to live at 250 O'Connor was unthinkable. He had not moved in officially but his constant presence was very much part of my new life with him.

23

Harassment at the Post Office

With a Bachelor of Education degree behind me and the inherent fall-back security it provided, I set out to find work in August of 1981. Teaching was out of the question, yet the opportunities were there and I eventually accepted an offer I couldn't refuse. In the days that I taught French as a second language, I envied my colleagues who had their own home rooms and taught the prescribed curriculum. Young kids aged 8 or 9 were, in my opinion, the easiest to reach; at that age, they are charming, inquisitive, smart, open to ideas and competitive. At times vulnerable, they could easily be molded to conform to acceptable standards.

When the principal of South Hull Elementary called and asked if I could take on a three-month assignment (maternity leave replacement) for a Grade 3 French Immersion class, the lure was too strong for me to resist. For the first month, I was in 7th heaven; the class size was acceptable, the student mix fascinating with many nationalities represented. It didn't take long for me to warm up to those beautiful young children so eager to learn and to please the teacher. To this day, I still don't know why I was not passionate about teaching; I completed the assignment and moved on.

At a crossroads of life, I looked for answers to my career dilemma; not interested in becoming a translator, not passionate about teaching, not smart enough to make it to Design School, the options were getting narrower. Damn, where did I go wrong?

One late December evening, I pulled myself away from the tube and went for a beer at a bar known as 166B. Feeling depressed because of lack of work, I knew I would need to make contacts to land my next gig. There were few gay bars in Ottawa at that time; 166B named after its civic address on Laurier West, was a dump, Dust balls hung from the stalactite ceiling, the placed reeked of stale beer and the washrooms were filthy. Yuck! The waiters were tired old men who had been let go when the bar on the lower level of the Lord Elgin closed its doors. The new hotel owners wanted to get rid of the silly old queens who frequented the place (and cruised the upstairs washrooms) to make the establishment respectable once again.

The 'B' as it was affectionately called attracted a wide variety of men and the odd woman who dared to venture in. Joshua piped up saying that he had been there one night with his then partner Mauricio and two of their friends. That evening, all four of them, dressed to the nines, had gone to Tactics in the Byward Market then headed to 166B. Looking around, they noticed that they were the youngest people in the place. Feeling overdressed and underwhelmed, they quickly downed the bottles of beer and left vowing never to go back.

Barry Turner was there on one cold December night. I could always count on him for intelligent conversation. That evening, I was in tatters; half crying, I made my case asking whether he knew of anyone who was looking to hire a good man. I told him I was ready to do *any* kind of work; I desperately needed income to pay for necessities. He made no promises but said that he would ask around; he worked in human resources for the Post Office. In the salary warrant directorate, there was always a need for additional staff, as employees moved on to better jobs once they had enough experience behind them. Barry knew that it was not an ideal work environment but I insisted that he talk to the Director General about me.

Within days, I was interviewed, screened for security purposes and hired into the salary warrants output division. My supervisor, a young man with an ego as big as the sun, assigned me to work in conjunction with Gayle Nestor, an experienced employee who was passionate about her work and kind towards me. She sensed that I was not in the right environment; what was a university-educated guy with two diplomas doing in an environment where the vast majority had only completed high school. Some of the colleagues in my unit were goons. They were ignorant regarding how to treat others with respect and I quickly became the target for what would and should have been considered harassment.

Each day right after reporting to work, the gang of macho men sat at their desks and shot the breeze about sports events they had watched the night before. As the supervisor came in later, this waste of time was never noticed. They took advantage of his absence to ridicule me in numerous ways. One of the guys had noticed that my car was Honda Civic DL. *'DL means dick licker!'* said Mike Maynard loud enough so that anyone on the floor could hear him. There was no point in saying anything; I'm sure my face turned beet red every time he uttered nonsense like this.

Bernie Merman, a Jewish women in her fifties, whose desk was very near our division, called me over to her cubicle; she was concerned about me and wanted me to know that she would do all she could to help me find another job somewhere in the government. A recovering alcoholic, she attended AA meetings and had met some senior government officials. She had learned about a new government program being set up to encourage oil and gas exploration in Canada. A few weeks later, she announced that she was leaving to work for the Petroleum Incentives Program at the Department of Energy, Mines and Resources.

It was shattering news for me; my world would continue a steady decline without the help and moral support of a person like Bernie. On her last day before leaving, she asked me for a copy of my resumé, which she intended to give to her new supervisor. With any luck, I might get interviewed, I thought. Several weeks went by before Jane Westin called asking to meet me concerning clerical jobs on offer in the Petroleum Incentives Program. Although legislation had not yet passed into law, the department was gearing up for the launch of the new program. Management was hiring and new people joined the organization every day.

My prayers were answered, thank God. I was transferred to a clerical position at the same occupational group and level (with identical pay) at the department of Energy, Mines and Resources. The Program offices were located in the West Memorial Building on Wellington Street just down from the Parliament Buildings. I felt such a sense of accomplishment by landing this low-level yet very secure and permanent position in the federal public service. The organization had become a crown corporation while I was working there, and staff mobility issues had begun to impact almost all employees. With this new job, the sky was the limit; I would be allowed to apply for any job anywhere in the federal government.

Four people had been hired to work as operational support staff. In addition to Bernie and I, there were two other people (Linda Shortt and Ron Kippling) in the unit reporting to Lucille Lemay. The four of us had virtually nothing to do as the program had not officially launched. We read books, played cards and goofed around to while away the hours. Anything was better than the harassment I had endured at the Post Office.

When Lucille came around to see how we were doing, I offered to do any work she could find for me. She eventually came back and offered us an opportunity to help the people working in the Management Consulting Team. They were behind in their work and needed someone who was willing to photocopy documents. There weren't many takers; in fact, I was the only one. Idle hands are the work of the devil, I thought to myself; better to be busy than bored! In time, another door opened thanks to my eagerness to work.

24

Meeting my Future Mother-in-Law

May 10th, 1992 was a pivotal day which I still vividly remember. I was under considerable stress; I was also excited to finally meet Josh's Mother. The invitation to dinner at Louisa and Sergio's home in Gatineau was a mixed blessing. Josh's father was in Asia on a two-week business trip leaving his mother alone on Mother's Day.

At the time, I would not have suspected that Joshua might have been involved in planning this fateful event. When Joshua told me that we had been invited to his sister's home on Mother's Day, I didn't immediately realize that I would be meeting his mother.

'Hey, you'll be meeting my mother at last!' said Josh. 'You've wanted to meet her and this is your chance. With my father away in China, there is no better opportunity.'

'Are you sure that he will be OK with that when he finds out?' I asked.

'Perhaps,' said Josh, 'but there is nothing he will be able to do about it at that point. If you're afraid that it might do more harm than good, then I suggest you not worry about it too much. My mother will make him see the light.'

'I feel this is all a little bit devious,' I countered.

'You have to take an opportunity when it presents itself,' Joshua continued.

'I hope this doesn't put a bigger wedge between your family and me,' I said. 'I would hate to have this chance encounter go sour on us. I'm also mindful that your father may make it difficult for you to move in with me. He may see this as an affront to his authority, a bold and disrespectful move he may not appreciate.'

'Chances are that things will flare up a bit when he hears of it; my mother will help smooth things over, I'm sure,' said Joshua confidently. 'Things will die down, don't worry.'

His coolness with what appeared to me as playing with fire was enough to settle my angst. One bad move and I could put our relationship in jeopardy. I would have to be very prim and proper if I was to make a good impression, one that would certainly be spoken about in the weeks to follow.

Nothing was left to chance. I did not want to jinx this special occasion which could not be repeated. One does not get a second chance to make a first impression. Remembering that Josh's mother had seen me briefly in February, I wondered how much she recalled from that short serendipitous encounter. I had ample time to prepare myself so that I wouldn't be putting my foot into my mouth, not that I did that very often; this special evening would mark the beginning of the first chapter in my dealings with my future in-laws and nothing was going to get in my way.

Whoever decided that the second Sunday in May would be Mother's Day was certainly in tune with nature; without fail, this day has always been a beautiful, bright and sunny time of the month. We arrived early. Sergio and Louisa's home had just been completed; high cathedral ceilings in the living room, a key feature, set the tone from the moment you set foot inside. A quick tour of the house gave me time to get my bearings which included knowing where the closest washroom was located just in case something unpredictable occurred. I felt a touch of paranoia enter my body but dismissed it as soon as I realized what was happening to me. Nerves, damn nerves!

We sat in the living room; Joshua and I shared the sofa. As I recall, there was no tension in the room. As we waited for the guest of honor to arrive, we drank white wine and talked about decorating plans for the house. The combination of the wine and informal discussion on decorating ideas, a subject with which I felt perfectly comfortable, helped reduce the anxiety I had about what was just about to begin. It's not the Spanish Inquisition I thought to myself; this is just a friendly meeting with someone who is eager to get to know me. *Calm down Richard*, I said to myself, Rome wasn't built in a day; as long as I don't make a fool of myself, this was going rather well.

Just then, the doorbell rang and the door opened. Josh's mother came in carrying bags bearing her contribution to the meal even if the occasion was in her honor. I was impressed at her thoughtfulness.

She was as beautiful as I had remembered her from the few minutes we had seen each other earlier in the year. Dressed in more casual clothing than when we first met, she wore a silk dress in a pink, off-white and black fabric. To complete the ensemble, she wore a black bolero styled jacket, a double string of black beads and patent leather black shoes. Her blonde hair was arranged in an upsweep leaving her forehead mostly visible with curls of blonde hair cascading down to the nape on either side of her head and at the back. For a 49 year old woman, she did not look her age; her flawless make-up had been applied to perfection. It was obvious that clothing and appearance mattered, and I was glad I had chosen to wear my best dress pants and designer shirt.

She sat at the opposite end of the sofa and focused on the centre of the room, not on me. I was grateful that she had the good sense to do that. Joshua had wisely decided to sit elsewhere; sitting next to me on the sofa might have been a bit forthright. With a glass of white wine in hand, she asked a few questions to find out more about me.

Food was brought out and placed on the square cocktail table in front of the couch. There was a plate of cheese, shrimps and sauce on a platter, cut vegetables and dip in a bowl and a basket of assorted crackers and bread. I was blending in as much as I could; the discussions included a range of topics. What was interesting to me was the speed in which each topic was covered; somebody would start talking about something to which others added their thoughts. In a flash, the conversation moved to the next story; you had to be quick to follow the flow and get a word in edgewise.

Without realizing it, I was being assessed in many ways. These were well-mannered people who spoke calmly and were respectful of each other. It wasn't very different from what I had experienced at home; I felt quite comfortable throughout the evening. I had been observed from many angles; there was enough information that could be gleaned from our conversation to allow a good analysis of this newcomer to the family.

That night, I suffered another major uveitis attack. I had been told that stress played a key role in the flare-ups. Everything was under control at work and my relationship with Joshua was smooth sailing. Maybe I underestimated the stress that I was going through while under the microscope.

A few weeks later, Louisa told Joshua that their father had been informed of the happenings on Mother's Day. He was not entirely pleased. Louisa repeated her father's exact words that concerned me: *he will never set foot in our house!* I was welcome in Sergio and Louisa's home but not at the family homestead.

Strong-willed men never say things they don't mean. I knew this was serious talk; there was no way around the barrier he had erected with those uncompromising words. My fear was not the fact that I could never be part of Josh's family; I was terrified that Joshua would see this as a sign that he should retreat and end the relationship. Thankfully, his reassurance came quickly. Joshua vowed not to spend Christmas in Florida with the family the following December. I wondered if those words had been said in all honestly or simply to make me feel secure amidst the turmoil of the hour.

25

Coming up in the World

Ever since I was a young boy in northern New Brunswick, I had wanted to write and publish. I'm not sure where this desire came from but it followed me to Ottawa when, in my first years in the city, a university professor suggested that I should publish short stories I had written for my second-language students. 'Audacious', I thought to myself; if I don't try, I'll never know whether or not this project could be successful. I struck it lucky with Gage Publications; their rejection letter was the softest letdown I'd ever see. Based on their review of the material submitted, they were willing to go forward with publication if the Government of Ontario provided deficit funding. Unfortunately, that never happened; later they suggested I approach other publishers which I did almost immediately. A small not-for-profit publication firm largely financed by the Ontario provincial government took interest and brought the project to fruition in the fall of 1982.

The stories formed a collection of children's books to be used as aids for phonetic learning. It started as an assignment while I was completing a Certificate of teaching French as a second language at l'Université du Québec à Hull. While in development, I had tested the short stories with my students at Gatineau Elementary. The kids were fascinated by the constant repetition of phonemes; one highlighted phoneme per book. The eight-book collection (Collection Turlututu) I launched in my hometown of Dalhousie, New Brunswick in front of a small crowd of friends and family members which included my mother, my sister Claire, my aunt Céline, my cousin Jeanette and a gaggle of ladies, all friends of the family.

My financials were much better than they had been; I was now able to take short trips every once in a while. My brother Phil had moved to Sarnia so I decided that I would take the train and spend the Easter weekend with him and his family.

Being together with them gave me the sense of grounding I needed.

On one trip to Toronto, I met up with my friend Shane and his new companion, Alonzo, whom I was meeting for the first time. It was a rather strange encounter as Shane and I had been an item in the early seventies and had remained friends. We had met at the Student Union Building of the Saint Francis Xavier University campus in Antigonish, Nova Scotia. We had bonded very quickly; Mireille Mathieu's music brought us together in many ways. Shane was a student while I worked as a manager trainee for the Canadian Imperial Bank of Commerce. After we parted ways, we kept in touch a few times a year; we enjoyed each other's company and arranged to meet when and where possible. When I heard that he had met Alonzo and that things were going very well, I was very happy for him. Shane deserved to be with a loving partner; Alonzo was everything he had wanted in a spouse.

In the winter of 1983, I bought my first color television: with a 14-inch screen, it was somewhat bulky requiring a deep shelf to accommodate it. Soon after I had arrived in Ottawa right in the middle of the teak craze, I bought a three-section wall unit. One of the units was specially made to house a television set. My new television sat perfectly in this cabinet. Most of my friends already had color TV but until that time, I just couldn't afford it. It was either I paid in cash or waited to have the money to make a purchase.

Not long afterwards, I appreciated it even more when I looked at the taping of an interview I did with Margaret Trudeau, the wife of the Prime Minister. I was a guest on Morning Magazine when we talked about the Collection Turlututu. The segment was very short; I don't remember much of it. What I recall with vivid clarity was the on-air wink Margaret gave me. I wasn't sure that the cameras had captured it, but when I went to work the following day, it was a hot topic around the water fountain. In appreciation of the exposure I had been given by this CTV segment, I autographed and sent a copy of the Collection to the Trudeau family at 24 Sussex Drive, the official residence.

Still feeling a bit high as a result of the interview with my favorite celebrity, I was quickly brought back down to reality with an eviction notice. The owner of 398 Chapel Street had sold the building and all the tenants had to vacate within 30 days. What a shock it was! I had lived there for the past five years; I had not given any thought to where I would want to live if ever I tired of the place or needed to move. I liked Sandy Hill, in part because of its proximity to the downtown core.

With a 3% vacancy rate, finding a rental unit in Ottawa in those days was not an easy task. You had to be quick on your feet, fast with your dialing finger and early to get to the viewing before the hordes got there ahead of you. Even getting the first appointment did not guarantee that the place would still be available when you arrived to see the place.

The trick to getting a good apartment was to buy the local newspapers as early in the day as possible, zero in on new listings, and make appointments the same day. The description for a one-bedroom apartment with two fireplaces and wood floors in a historic house on Besserer Street made me bounce out of my chair. There was even parking included. The woman who answered the phone seemed like a very refined and sophisticated lady. She told me that I was the first to call; she also would consider potential tenants in the order that the calls were received. She urged me to come and visit without delay. Sensing that this would be *the* apartment of my dreams, I dressed the part. I figured that the owners would carefully select a new tenant as they lived on the first floor of this elegant residence.

What I found out from Mrs. Diellar was equally fascinating and surprising. Their house had been built by Sir Sandford Fleming for his daughter as a wedding gift. Located at the back end of the garden, the house faced Besserer Street while the Fleming row house was on Daly Street. 410 Besserer had been divided into four apartments. The Diellars occupied all of the ground floor of this huge stone house with white columns and leaded stained-glass windows. Two apartments share the second story and a small unit had been built in the attic of the house. The vacant unit was the front half of the second story.

For a one-bedroom apartment, this was a big unit boasting a large living room with a working fireplace. The kitchen had been added over the front porch below. It was small yet big enough for a table and two chairs. Behind the living room, there was the dining room with a fireplace that had been condemned years ago. The bedroom across the hallway had been built where the staircase once had been. A clothes closet had been added to the outer wall such that one third of the huge hallway stain glass window was in fact inside the walk-in. The window continued into the bedroom.

I had to contain my excitement; I was afraid that they would increase the rent on the spot if they knew how much I wanted the apartment. I filled in the application and within 24 hours, it was confirmed that I could move in during the first week of May.

Provincetown was in the cards that year; Norman and I made the long trek together while his spouse Leon drove down with other friends. It had become an annual Labor Day ritual that had started years earlier with Jean Bélair. We'd arrive for the start of the long weekend and enjoy the frenzy of the season finale. By Monday afternoon, the village was much more quiet as people left to go back home in time for work on Tuesday morning. Now almost deserted, the previously crowded streets seemed somewhat dull in comparison.

Over the next five days, our routine consisted of breakfast on the deck, lunch at the beach at Race Point, cocktails at 4 on the deck, tea dance at the Boatslip at 5, and dinner at 7:30 in one of the fancy restaurants around town. An obligatory after-dinner walk was required to digest the copious amounts of food. We walked the length of Commercial Street going in and out of novelty stores, clothing boutiques, book and antique shops, and art galleries. There were enough businesses open in the evening that we managed to find new places to visit every night. It was a visual treat; store owners, mostly gay men, were adept at displaying merchandize in the most tantalizing ways possible.

26

Transitions

At times, it was difficult for me to contain the joy I had by being with Joshua, not that I had to refrain when he was around. It was all the sadness that surrounded us at the time that made me feel that I was 'too lucky for my own good'. Josh's grandmother was very ill with leukemia, Chris (my friend Dave's partner in Montréal) had a benign brain tumor removed, and my good friend Birdie had been told that she had four months to live. All of this would have been easier to take had it not been for the myriad of close friends who were either HIV positive or had full blown AIDS with countless symptoms.

Joshua was about to turn 30 in a few weeks; I could sense this wasn't a happy time for him. Every year on his birthday, he got depressed or so he told me. To help lift his mood, we went and made our travel arrangements for the fall trip to Europe.

To add to the misery, Louisa's June wedding was fast approaching and Joshua was tense. It would have been totally inappropriate for me to be there as Josh's partner when, in fact, I had not met any of the relatives and friends who would be attending. There would be time in the years that followed to meet Josh's relatives in a more congenial environment.

Ironically, I too was invited to a wedding to which Joshua would not be attending. My brother Danny called to ask me if I would agree to be an usher at his wedding the following November. I attended the nuptials in Fredericton on my own.

Quietly, I started emptying out drawers to make room for Josh. For the first time in my life, I would be sharing my accommodations; something I had wanted for a long time but the thought of it terrified me. What will happen if it doesn't work? Would compromises be difficult?

Making space for Joshua was helping me come to terms with the end of a long chapter of my life; living alone since

1978, I had certainly taken on certain habits that would be difficult to break, not the least of which was being a pack rat. Similar to those people who had lived in the 1930s when scarcity of food and supplies were at the highest point, parting with anything useful was a sacrilege worthy of being reported at confession time. While I made room for Josh, I purposely found new places to stash things which I could not, or would not, part. Thus, the cavities behind each piece of furniture and the far reaches of the closets were used to store innumerable 'things' of dubious use.

A mere thirteen days before Louisa's wedding, the paternal grandmother passed away. There was sadness in Josh's eyes though he held back the flood of tears that he later shed in private in the washroom. My sadness came from the fact that I would never have the pleasure of meeting her. She had been such an important part of Josh's life; it would have been revealing to know her. She left with very few warning signs; perhaps she felt that her illness would put a damper on the special occasion. Days later, it was confirmed that she had felt unwell and would not have wanted the focus to be on her.

The frequency and severity of the uveitis in my right eye started to recede; I discovered the benefits of acupuncture as a complementary treatment. To my surprise and amazement, the relief, albeit temporary, was a step in the right direction. My body was healing in ways it had not done so before. The weight on my shoulders had been removed when I left the management position I had occupied for almost two years. And though my boss Joanna cried when I announced my imminent departure from her division, I had no remorse whatsoever. She had been part of the problem all along. A perfectionist with a strong sense of duty, it had never occurred to her that my health issues had been compounded by the stress, created in part by her wish to impress her boss. Never before had I noticed the direct correlation between my level of stress and the number and intensity of my uveitis attacks. I controlled it or it controlled me; I definitely wanted to win this battle but it would take many more years to get a handle on it.

Before starting the new job, I decided to make a trip to Dalhousie to see my father. He had called to say that my sister Claire and my brother Danny would be visiting in early July and that it would be great if I could be there at the same time. Annamaria, Danny's bride-to-be, was also going to be in Dalhousie. As I had not yet met her, this was a good opportunity for me to get to know her before the wedding.

My father's failing health was reason enough to travel to Dalhousie; he was getting frail and it would be a matter of months before he would need to be placed in a home. Back home in New Brunswick, Geoffrey's health was also very precarious; he was holding on but it was evident that it took all of his strength to keep from letting go. There was no getting away from illness; it surrounded me whether I was in Ottawa or in Dalhousie. My health issues in comparison were minor; I dared not complain about my situation in the presence of others who suffered much more than I did.

When the good Lord closes a door, somewhere he opens a window. For me, that was Josh's presence in my life. Dark as it was in those days, Josh's lightness and comfort was enough to get me through these times unscathed.

27

The Burlington Get-away

Cabin fever in February is an annual occurrence with me and 1984 was no exception. Getting through winter without a break is like running a 10k marathon without a bottle of water. I was determined to get out of town; a change is as good as a rest, I thought to myself. It didn't have to be a trip to an exotic location; it just had to offer a new horizon, something different from the everyday routine.

My fondness for car trips under four hours helped me focus on possibilities. Using a compass and centering the pivot on Ottawa, there were limitless possibilities for short excursions but many destinations offered very little appeal. American destinations were more alluring. 'Burlington, Vermont it is,' I said to myself.

'The purpose of your trip?' asked the Border Patrol agent. 'Skiing', Norman replied. 'We'll be renting our equipment in Burlington', Norman quickly added as he noticed the frown on the officer's face.

'Do you really think he believed us?' I said. 'There's not an ounce of snow on the ground, and we come without any equipment whatsoever.'

'Well, we're in the US now,' said Norman. 'The main thing is that we crossed into Vermont without trouble. He'll never know our real reason for coming here.'

'Why did we come here?' I said jokingly.

'Just drive and shut up,' Norman said as he looked straight ahead towards the rolling hills of Vermont. 'What's in Burlington?'

'Not much,' I replied. 'There is one gay bar we should check out. With our luck, it will be closed or moved to a new unknown location.'

'Let's be positive,' said Norman. 'This is an adventure. Whatever happens, happens. It's unlikely that prince charming lives in Burlington but we'll never know unless we go looking.'

'I've given up on long distance relationships, especially cross-border ones,' I said. 'For the most part, American men are charming; even the poster boy for Camel cigarettes wouldn't be enough for me to want to start another affair with a foreigner.'

'Do you think you'll ever find someone that will meet your expectations?' asked Norman.

'I realize I've set very high standards for a partner,' I said. 'For a long-term relationship to work there has to be a lot more than physical attraction. *Beauty is more than skin deep* as my Mother used to say. Until the day that I find the right person, I'll live alone. If it takes years, then so be it. If it never happens, I'll live with the consequences.'

Unbeknownst to me, people in Ottawa thought I was 'way too picky'. I had a reputation! My parents had always insisted on the 'best' in everything. Nothing less would be acceptable in my book, I was raised that way. Watching Jayne Torvill and Christopher Dean skating to the music of "Bolero" at the winter Olympics and getting perfect 6s, it struck me that for two people to be so close together, the synchronization had to be flawless. I viewed relationships much in the same way. As in 'Bolero', the tempo starts off quite slowly and builds up. Life would unfold in the same manner but would be easier if partners were well matched.

We approached Burlington within an hour of crossing the border. Without knowing which of the many exits to take, we chose the one that said 'Downtown'. At about 4 pm, we found the gay bar we were looking for based on information found in an old Damaron Gay Guide. It was closed but there were people inside — musicians practicing for a performance no doubt. Our presence at the front door did not go unnoticed. A young man came to greet us and informed us that the bar was scheduled to open at 6 pm. He explained that there was live entertainment in the evening; we should come back and see their show. When we enquired whether this was a gay bar, we were told that the place was under new management; it was no longer attracting that clientele. He directed us to another bar in the downtown core.

Back in the car, we drove to the motel where we had booked a room. On the way, I commented on the young man's good looks to which Norman acquiesced. We quickly unpacked then set out to find a decent restaurant in the heart of the city. We made our way to Pearl Street, one of the main arteries in downtown Burlington. There was ample parking at Cathedral Square; we left the car there and walked along Pearl until we found a non-descript family restaurant.

We lingered in the café far too long, but we weren't asked to leave. It was way too early to go looking for the new gay bar that had recently opened on the second floor of an establishment at 109 Pearl Street. The young man we had met earlier had assured us that it was the in-place to go in Burlington; there were no other options.

The Pearl Street Bar was mostly empty when we arrived. The crowd started to fill the place after 11 pm. We stood at the bar drinking beer and observing the locals. Every once in a while, inquisitive eyes would focus on us. Were we that obvious? Did it say 'foreigner' on our foreheads? Or were we 'fresh meat' in a town where most people are stale to one another?

In a crowd, Norman stood out; his smile and beautiful blonde hair attracted attention wherever he went. He was bait! Maybe he was too attractive; he could intimidate even the boldest. But we stood alone; not one person came to chat with us.

Just as we were talking about leaving, the young musician from the other bar walked in. He spotted us within seconds and made a beeline to where we were standing.

'Hi, my name is Justin. I met you earlier at the other bar. I thought I'd see you guys at one of our performances!' he said.

'My name is Richard and my friend is Norman,' I said. 'Sorry, we weren't quite sure we would find the place after dark. We made our way to Pearl Street to find a place to eat not far from here.'

'Where are you guys from?' Justin asked.

'We're Canadians from Ottawa,' Norman answered. 'Sorry to have missed your show. Did you get many people?'

In the following minutes, we heard that Justin was performing with his sister Sheila in various locations in New England. They had a small following of admirers. As with any musical groups, their hope was to make it big; in Nashville or elsewhere. Burlington had not been a great success but nevertheless, they had been paid to perform even though not many people showed up for their two performances.

The more I listened to Justin, the more I was intrigued by this young man with so much energy and drive. Masculine yet sensitive, all of his attention was on us. He was interested in knowing why we had made the trip to Vermont. For once we didn't have to give a geography lesson to an American; he knew a lot more about Canada than most of his countrymen. He had never been to Ottawa but he had visited Montréal and Toronto on several occasions.

Slowly, people left the bar as it was getting late. I signaled to Norman that it was time to leave; Justin picked up on my non-verbal cue and asked where we were staying.

Our room was just a few doors down from theirs at the Travelodge. Till the wee hours of the morning, Justin and I talked. He was very open and sincere about his life, his family, his aspirations, and his dream of making it into the big league. I felt myself falling for an American once again; it was hard for me to refrain. Holding back had never been easy for me; Justin was the epitome of a man on the road to success and I wanted to ride on his coat-tails.

28

Broken 'Gaydar'

Joshua met my brother Phil who was in Ottawa for a weekend. They hit it off well as I had expected they would.

Phil was going through a hard time; separation was imminent. He needed to talk and I listened and supported him throughout the conversations we had. Life had been good to him up until then; he had not imagined that one day he would reach the point of no return in a relationship that had been so strong from the start. Devastated by the sad turn of events, he cried for short periods before regaining composure. He felt he had failed; for a person used to being in the top percentile of everything he tried, this was proving to be his holy grail.

Growing up, Phil demonstrated all the skills necessary to succeed. I was in awe of his abilities to reach every goal he set. He had become the one to follow, to emulate. My parents were very proud of their first child; he rarely let them down. Mature before his time and wise as an owl, he seemed to have it all. I ached for him. It was difficult for me to see him go through what was definitely his first major setback. 'Would he see it as a failure or as an undesirable event in his, thus far, unblemished existence? If falling in love can lead to foolish things, falling out of love could also lead to unwise or unhealthy choices. My bet was that he would be back on his feet after a period of mourning.

At about the same time as Phil's breakup, my best friend Mary, who had recently separated from her spouse Rocky, whispered to me that she thought she was lesbian. My initial reaction was one of shock. Mary and I had met ten years prior; we had become good friends. I thought I knew her well, but this revelation was one 'helluva' big surprise.

'You're not serious,' I said.

'Yes,' Mary answered. 'I've been reading a lot about gay life; I am more and more convinced that I'm gay!'

'Could have fooled me', I said. 'Not once have I ever thought you might be a lesbian. Your relationship with Ricardo was a bumpy ride but I was sure that only men could interest you.'

'I'm not saying that I'm not interested in men,' added Mary, 'all I'm saying is that a relationship with a woman would be so much simpler.'

'Surely, you're not turning to women simply because it would make for easier relationships?' I enquired.

'It's just an added benefit. I really don't know for sure if a relationship with another woman would work; I'm willing to give it a try if I find the right person,' said Mary with newfound confidence.

Shit! I thought my 'gaydar' was operational. How could I have missed this? How would her son and daughter handle this?

When you think you've experience it all, the guy up there sends you more new stuff to deal with. Death, disease, separation, divorce and seemingly straight people going gay were a bit more than I could handle. Thank God Joshua was in the picture. I could stand next to him and feel solid ground under us. He was my foundation at a time when I needed it most.

Good news came in the form of an electronic message (long before emails) that my new supervisor had agreed to the one-month leave I had requested so that Joshua and I could take that trip to Europe. This approval confirmed that it was now a done deal and that nothing could stop us from making it happen unless Josh's father found a way to put the kibosh on our plans. As there were no indications that such a move was being contemplated, it appeared that we had a green light for our travels.

Mary had started taking steps to see first hand what the gay community was up to in Ottawa. She persuaded me to take her to Centretown Pub on Somerset Street. Though mostly a male bastion of oversexed and undersupplied individuals, the place was alive with all kinds of people the night we decided to go. It was unusual to see women in the place but that evening Mary was able to check out a few smart-looking ladies. She was taken aback by the variety of types and styles; lesbians did not all fit the same mold. Some were masculine, some were feminine; some were dressed for barn work while others were very preppy. From no make up to full makeup, the gamut of choices was astonishing.

In walked Michael who spotted me sitting next to Mary. After the customary introductions, Michael told me that his new soulmate, Henry from New York City, had died in hospital three weeks after being admitted. He was visibly shaken by Henry's passing. They had met in the spring and had begun a long distance relationship that seemed to be going well. In those early days of AIDS, many did not have a chance to survive; by the time they were diagnosed, the illness had progressed to a point of no return. AZT, the preferred medication at the time, did not prevent death; it prolonged the agony without any significant benefits.

In comparison, my health issues were minor although they didn't seem that inconsequential to me at the time. Losing my sight as a result of multiple uveitis flare-ups was not acceptable. I became a regular at the Ottawa Eye Institute. In early August when the humidity can be smoldering, I had another bout of uveitis. Early warning signs were easy to notice; the white of the eye became pink and a feeling of sand particles in the eye made it difficult to feel comfortable. I rushed to the Eye Institute; I was seen by Dr. Zable who within minutes of checking my eye pressure decided that I needed an injection. Not a problem, I'm not afraid of needles. Then he explains that there will be a freezing agent on the eyeball so that I don't feel the needle! *Shit, you've got to be kidding,* I said to myself. I had no idea that a person could be administered an injection in the eye.

Recuperation time is about 12 hours; I slept most of it. I had taken all of the 222s they had offered. Hopefully, this would never happen again.

29

Another Forced Move

Not again! On Easter Monday, 1984, a note had been left on my door; 410 Besserer had been sold and the new owners wanted all tenants to vacate no later than August 1. Nothing had been said to me when I moved in the previous year in May that the building might be put up for sale. Had I known, I would probably have chosen to live elsewhere; moving was not my idea of fun.

Given that the owners were an older couple, I concluded that they had to sell because of health reasons or that they preferred not to have the responsibility for such a large piece of real estate. Regardless of the reason for the sale, it was very disappointing; finding suitable accommodations in Ottawa had always been a nightmare and during the time I had lived on Besserer Street, availability rates for rentals had dropped to the point where finding an apartment was akin to finding a needle in a hay stack.

Faced with the grim prospects of locating an apartment with character, in a good location and at a reasonable monthly rate, I considered ownership for the first time. With the help of a very patient real estate agent, I looked at all kinds and types of properties on the market. The advice I was getting led me to think that an income property was my only hope of purchasing something affordable. With nary a skill to fix anything that could go wrong in any one of the rental units, I soon realized that this option made no sense at all. My only hope was to buy small and away from the downtown core to which I was so strongly attracted.

Dyanne, my trusted and faithful realtor, convinced me to consider condo townhouses. What on earth would ever possess a single gay man to buy a row house in suburbia amongst a sea of heterosexuals?

My meager savings which had been set aside for an eventual trip to Europe with my friend André had to be used for the down payment. I had been looking forward to this trip for a while; André was a savvy traveler and joining him on my first voyage outside of North America would have given me the degree of safety I had yearned for. It was all for naught. There would be no trip to Europe; finding suitable accommodations became my top priority, frivolity would have to wait.

Michael had encouraged and supported me throughout the bidding process; in his opinion, real estate was the key to accumulating wealth. When I finally did acquire unit 102 at 3260 Southgate Road, he was more excited than I was, vowing to help me move in. Every available penny had been used up for the down payment; I had no funds to cover moving costs. Michael rounded up a team of friends and within a few hours, all of my belongings were in the townhouse.

After everyone had left, I sat and cried. What had I done? It had looked so pretty when I came to see it during the open house! The master bedroom had been painted 'hot pink'; I'd have to live with it as I could not afford to start renovating the place. The longer I stayed in that house, the more I realized that I had made a serious mistake.

The condo layout was standard. Upon entering the house, the main floor hallway had stairs to the right. To the left was the kitchen and from the kitchen, there was access to the dining room. At the end of the hallway, spanning the full width of the unit was the living room which opened up to the dining room. All three rooms on the ground floor had large windows looking into a small postage-stamp enclosed yard where nothing could grow; the tall trees on the other side of the fence provided a lot of shade but made for very dull natural light inside. On the second level, all three bedrooms also had windows on the side facing the yard and were arranged as in a mobile trailer all in a row. This place would never make it to the pages of Architectural Digest!

During the month of August, my mother and father came to visit bearing housewarming gifts. I had finally settled down; the presents may have been a way of telling me that they were proud that I had made a huge financial commitment in exchange for safety, security and a long-term investment.

Owning your home had always been the right thing to do; they had never been renters as they built their first house just as they got married. My father had few if any handyman skills, yet was able to maintain a house for many years. I hadn't learned much from him other than the ability to find the right people to fix whatever needed attention.

At Norman's urging, at the end of August, we drove to Dalhousie for a serendipitous weekend. He was long overdue for a visit with his family and had insisted that I come along with him, arguing the fact that my parents were going off on a European trip where there was always a chance for unexpected and unpleasant outcomes. Fearing the worst, I agreed to join him for the long drive back to the Maritimes. My unannounced visit was a success and I came home feeling good about it.

To get downtown from my townhouse took 20 to 25 minutes; there were no direct routes. Friends complained about the amount of time required getting to my place, and slowly they stopped coming. My isolation was getting the better of me. Within a year, I had put the place up for sale and moved back to 'civilization'. I never looked back on that year in the 'burbs'. The one good thing to come of it was that I now had savings which were carefully invested for the future.

Once again, I could afford to travel; within weeks of the closing, Norman and I were on our way for our annual trip to Provincetown. I hadn't been able to make that trip the previous year because of the financial commitments tied to the house. All of that was in the past; I had found a wonderful apartment right in the core of the city. I would be moving in just after the Cape Cod holiday.

Every trip to P-town was eventful; there were always plenty of surprises. What made this trip particularly great was our stop in West Yarmouth to visit with Justin who we had met in Burlington, and his sister Sheila who were performing there. It was a happy reunion made even more special because we got to meet their parents who had come down to see their show. Sheila's daughter, Laurie, was also with them. A beautiful and loving child, we took to her instantly.

Halloween is to gays what Christmas is to children. Not one for costumes myself, every year I turned down invitations to parties when dressing up was mandatory. Norman was at the opposite end of the spectrum; he loved putting on a frock every time there was an occasion to do so. He had done drag over the years; he had even talked Leon in joining him. Together they bought incredible evening gowns and dressed the part on several occasions. With his hairstyling and make-up skills, in a few hours, Norman could transform himself into an attractive woman. His transformations were so convincing that he won first prize at a Sacs Halloween party dressed as Her Majesty Queen Elizabeth II. He had researched every detail, sewn each stitch on his elegant ballroom off-white gown and coiffed his wig to look exactly like the Queen. It was as he called it 'A queen looking like The Queen!'

At Norman's insistence, I finally relented and agreed to do full drag, if only once in my lifetime. He was in charge of finding all the necessary props; there was no way I was volunteering to do that. He was excited about the prospects; a fortrel polyester beige and black knee length dress was bought at the Salvation Army store. There was no problem getting a wig as he was a hair stylist and had many stashed away in a trunk. Only the shoes were a problem. The Saint Vincent de Paul Thrift Store was well known for large sized shoes according to Coco Paradise; Norman found exactly the size I needed. At 6 pm on Halloween night, the make-over began. Everything went well until it was time for the make-up; when Norman started applying the layers that would eventually give a new look, it was the feel of the guck on my face that I found most unpleasant. When he had finally finished the job, I looked into the mirror and was amazed. I didn't look like myself; others would not guess it was me unless I opened my mouth. On our way to a party which was held in the basement of a friend's home, we drove to pick up a few other people. The comments were positive but I felt that I looked like a whore.

I soon realized that the fact that I couldn't be identified gave me a new identity free to do with it as I wanted. I chose to follow the look Norman had given me; naughty would be my theme for the night. I did things I would never have done without the disguise. It was so enjoyable to be a different person if only for a few short hours. I had done things that weren't proper when I had had a drink or two too many but in those cases, people knew me and weren't impressed with my mischievous behavior. This was very different. It all made sense to me now why people chose to do drag; it's a wonderful escape from reality with few consequences. If having fun meant that one wanted this kind of temporary change, who was I to question it? My views on people who did drag radically changed over the next few days.

30

A Forbidden Place

When a person says that you will never set foot in their house, you believe it. Josh's father had been unequivocal. There was no way he was having me as a guest in the family homestead. That was a touch painful but I decided that I wouldn't lose sleep over it. There was nothing I could do about it; Joshua was also powerless.

So when the invitation came from Joshua to a BBQ at his parent's home, I was sure he was joking.

'You can't be serious Josh,' I said

'I am serious,' he said. 'My parents are away and they won't know that you were in the house'.

'Isn't this a tad dangerous?' I added. 'What if they have a change of plans and come back home earlier than expected?'

'They are out of town for the weekend. I don't expect them back until Sunday evening,' said Josh. 'When they go to Québec City, they stay the full weekend. They have many friends there and they really enjoy the charming old city.'

When you live in an apartment and someone invites you to a BBQ, it's a real treat. Joshua had decided on steaks served with scalloped potatoes and green beans. I didn't know it then, but I would learn much later that this was a meal his mother made quite often. It fascinated me that he was such an expert at cooking on a BBQ, something I knew nothing about. I was charmed by Josh's social graces and his culinary abilities. The BBQ went without a hitch.

Our departure date for Europe was getting closer as each week went by. I sensed that Joshua was getting nervous about the trip; it was not so much what he said that triggered the alarms, it was his lack of the calmness that had always been there before. I hadn't pegged him as a nervous type; he was always in full control. Yet this extended voyage did seem to affect him in ways that I couldn't quite figure out. Asking him outright about his worries would probably yield a blank stare. In the end, I decided that whatever was nagging him was his business, not mine.

Together, we looked at storage units for Josh's music collection. We searched on line and in local stores to find cabinets to house his huge collection of CDs, books, and LPs. To my surprise, our tastes were very similar; we liked the same styles and were attracted to the same colors. That made it easy for us to plan our 'den' (our guest bedroom) which housed Josh's music collection along with the stereo equipment and television. In terms of square footage, this room was larger than the room I had chosen to use as the master bedroom, as natural light was better in the smaller of the two.

With each decision that we made, I felt that much closer and more connected to Josh. Although he hadn't yet moved in, it was in my best interest to involve him in every decision with regards to placement of furniture. In a way, I was letting go and allowing him to take his rightful place in what was to become our home for another 13 years, although at the time we had no idea how long we would stay at 250 O'Connor.

In my early days as a Staffing Consultant at the Public Service Commission, I finally learned to take it easy even as

I worked hard and the pace was grueling. My co-workers, many of whom were employees at the same level, were all very enjoyable and friendly. A major project was initiated at the time I arrived in the work unit; all employees were required to get involved. A change of employment legislation required that training sessions be provided to operational staff in all government departments so that they could apply the new regulatory framework. We were required to design the training materials and then deliver the sessions from Halifax to Vancouver. It was a mammoth task requiring eight to ten months of work.

Finally, I was in a job that suited me perfectly. It was heaven. I had fewer and less intense bouts of uveitis. Even my eczema had cleared up, the first time in over 20 years.

Joshua was also doing interesting work at the time. He was designing homes to be built by one of his father's many companies. Every night, he'd arrive with floor plans; we would sit together and I'd give him my comments based on my interior design skills. When a layout of a room made it difficult to do a reasonable and workable floor plan, we analyzed it to see what could be done to improve the flow by changing door-ways, adding or deleting walls or parts thereof. Without realizing it, we were subconsciously designing a home for ourselves. We never spoke about it; we knew that home ownership was a far-off vision. Was he dreaming of the same things I was?

31

Return to Civilization

The search for downtown accommodations commenced the minute I found out that the townhouse had sold. Like a kid in a candy store, I considered a number of available units most of which were more expensive than I could afford. I settled on a two-bedroom apartment on the first floor of an older house on Gilmour near Bay. On the second floor were two small one-bedroom apartments. Coming at it from the east, this white gabled house looked like it had been there for years and now in need of some TLC. A wrap-around veranda just outside my apartment and dormer windows on the second level gave it an old world charm that I found appealing. The back yard was large enough to accommodate several cars; this was of paramount importance when renting in the core of the city.

I was excited about moving back downtown but not overly thrilled with the apartment I was about to move into. It was affordable no doubt but lacked the refinement of 410 Besserer. Few buildings would ever compare with the sheer elegance of that historic building. Finding something similar was unthinkable, particularly at the end of summer when students are back in the city and have rented most if not all of the decent places in town.

Norman's encouraging words helped me to some extent. 'You did wonders with that dingy apartment at 398 Chapel, you'll make this new place look *maaaarvolous!'* His confidence in my skills was reassuring; however, it wasn't the prestigious apartment I had hoped for.

On my way to an appointment in the Medical Building at the corner at MacLaren and O'Connor streets, I noticed an older three storey walk-up that had been renovated. Out of curiosity, I went in to see the model suite located in the south east corner on the second floor. What struck me immediately were the gleaming hardwood floors, the coved ceilings and the leaded windows in every room including kitchen and bathroom. I asked if the model suite was still available and to my surprise it was. The real shocker was the rental fee, significantly more than the apartment I had rented on Gilmour.

The rooms were spacious especially the living room and dining room. The one drawback was the tiny galley kitchen, a concession I was more than willing to endure for the pleasure of being in luxurious surroundings. I found myself thinking about living at 250 O'Connor. Just the address seemed more appealing to me than the 518 Gilmour. Connor Court had a regal resonance to its name; my mother had always teased us about being from royal blood. This would be as close as I would get to living a regal life!

Michael would help me decide if this was a good move; he knew real estate and was financially astute. He would tell me if this made sense or if I was dreaming in technicolour. I explained to him my dilemma. How was I going to get out of a signed lease agreement? As there were many other people wanting the same apartment, the owner agreed to offer it to the next person on his list without charging me for any expenses he may have incurred. I was very grateful to him.

As expected, Michael had all the answers. In a matter of minutes, he had drawn a sure fire plan of action that would address all of my concerns. He was convinced that I would not want to move out of 250 O'Connor anytime soon, and that alone would be a money saver as I typically went from one place to another every three or four years costing me a small fortune every time. That kind of forward thinking was not natural to me, yet Michael's ability to do so helped me many times over. His business management skills impressed me; if I remained friends with him, maybe his skills would rub off on me, or least that's what I was hoping.

On Saturday, September 14th 1985, I moved to 250 O'Connor, apartment 11. Once all of the furniture and boxes had been unloaded, I opened a bottle of champagne to celebrate; *Here's to my new apartment on this, my 33rd birthday!*

Living downtown meant that I was close to many of my friends and acquaintances. It was so much easier to plan outings even at the last minute. My friend Luke, who also sang in the Ottawa Men's Chorus, lived just down the street on

MacLaren. On Tuesday nights, I'd call on him on my way to choral practice. A dear and trusted friend, Luke was a shy French Canadian from Moose Creek. He was as slim as a man could be without looking ill. His blue eyes and broad smile were his trademarks; he knew many in the gay community for his kindness towards others was ubiquitous.

I met Jonathan Garbo at a Christmas wine and cheese party held by my choral mate Luke. There was an instant connection to this beautiful man with a birthday on September 15th. Both Virgos, we had much in common; perhaps too much in common to make a relationship work over a long period. From the start, my gut feeling was that a relationship with Jonathan would be difficult; he was strong willed, very attractive and non committal about the long term. I sensed that he had not finished sowing his wild oats: I was going to get hurt.

Throwing caution to the wind, I decided that whatever could come from even a short-term affair was better than no relationship at all, and so I put my heart and soul into this emerging liaison that had all the signs of not being too solid. It was a lop-sided union; I was in love with him regardless of whether or not he was in love with me. I was going for broke; there was no stopping me.

Jonathan could best be described as a German hunk; good looking, intelligent, comical and yet serious, resourceful and impeccably dressed. He possessed that Germanic sense of style and good taste which he used in all facets of his life. Methodical to a fault, he was a true Virgo, a perfectionist in all things.

My annual trek to Dalhousie at Christmastime was emotionally draining; it had been a year since my mother had passed away. There was little joy in my father's house; it took every bit of energy to make it through the Holidays. Christmas would never be the same again; my Mother had been the nucleus of the family.

The five-day stay in Dalhousie was as much as I could stand. I was anxious to get back to Ottawa, back to civilization. A huge party hosted by Dwayne Warnock on New Year's Eve was billed as the social event of the season; I was looking forward to it.

32

Autumn is for Virgos

The Gatineau Hot Air Balloon Festival was a sure sign that summer was coming to a close. Held every year over the Labor Day weekend, balloon enthusiasts from all over America and even a few from Europe come to this beautiful and colorful event. Joshua was proud to be my guide on my first visit to the Festival. As a Member of Parliament for Gatineau, Joshua's father was on the festival site every morning; it was unavoidable that we would meet him on the grounds. The chance encounter was brief and polite; after all he was a politician and as all politicians do so well, they greet people with all due dignity regardless of their interest in whom they are meeting. Even if I had known little about this man, I would have been impressed by his presence. Tall, attractive and well spoken, he had a keen sense of what was happening around him at all times. He knew who I was, having heard my name, and seen my picture on Josh's night stand in Florida. A day or two later, I met him again in the VIP tent along with Joshua's maternal grandmother. A bit more relaxed this time, I sensed that he was more comfortable being out of sight from prying and inquisitive eyes.

'Isn't this your favorite time of the year?' asked Josh.

'You bet,' I said. 'I was born in the fall; harvest time for me means a season of thanksgiving for the bounty of fruit and vegetables from the land. Every year, at this time, I go to the Byward Market and get a variety of vegetables and fresh herbs to make a vegetarian spaghetti sauce.'

'You make spaghetti sauce without meat?' said Josh with a touch of sarcasm. 'I can't imagine it without ground beef.'

'You will, in time,' I said. 'I make a huge batch of it every September and freeze it in double portions which lasts me for a year. On average, once a week, I have a meal of pasta with my primavera sauce. It can also be used to make lasagna.'

'No meatless lasagna for me!' said Josh. 'I'll have my mother make us some pasta sauce with beef. 'What vegetables and herbs do you put in your sauce?' Joshua enquired.

'It depends on what's available but usually includes tomatoes, peppers, celery, onions, string beans, zucchini, eggplant, broccoli, cauliflower, carrots, mushrooms, anise bulb, scallions and leeks. Fresh herbs typically include basil, dill, chives and tarragon. To spike it up, I add garlic, red wine and Tabasco sauce to the tomato base.'

'Where did you find the recipe?' asked Josh.

'Didn't find it; I made it up!' I said. 'It's never the same from year to year as I alter the proportions or I omit some of the vegetables I normally use.'

'How long having you been doing this,' asked Josh.

'The tradition started not long after I arrived in Ottawa,' I said. 'I had several good reasons; by having a ready-made meal that I could pull out from the freezer meant that I didn't need to make meals every day of the week; produce in the fall is very inexpensive, specially if you go to the Market when they open up at 6:30 am, the vendors are far more generous at that time of day. Because of my arthritis, I had focused on eating more fruit and vegetables and less red meat.'

'Not sure I'm going to like this sauce,' said Josh, 'but I'm willing to give it a try.'

It was quite a production; I made on average 40 to 60 portions. Rising at 6 am, I'd be out the door carrying as many shopping bags as I needed, heading to the Market in my car. The weight of the bags left me no choice but to use my vehicle despite the fact that the market was within walking distance from my apartment.

Walking up and down the length of the Byward Market square where the vendors were located, I checked out what was on offer and at what price. I compared the quality of products from one seller to the next so that I would get the best value for the money. Once my initial inspection was completed, I started at the South end of the Square and stopped at pre-selected stalls. When the bags got too heavy, I made a dash to the car to unload what I had bought thus far. Returning to where I had left off, I continued my route until I had completed my purchases.

To make it easier on the vendors, I always carried a bagful of coins so that the transactions could be completed quickly. Most of the farmers were French Canadians from eastern Ontario; I enjoyed talking to them about their produce and their stamina to get going so early in the morning. In no time at all, they set up an empty stall with imagination and style. I'm sure these people have never seen the inside of a design /merchandizing school but they sure knew how to showcase their wares.

Europe! In a few weeks we'll be on our way. One minute I was excited, the next, worried. I came up with a mild case of 'what ifs'. What if we get on each other's nerves? What if he finds things out about me that he can't live with? What if he wants to cut the trip short? I feared that Joshua would give up on me and end the relationship in a fit of panic. A less drastic outcome would be the postponement of our co-habitation allowing him more time to decide.

It would have been difficult to be on one's best behavior for a solid month; Joshua would certainly see my true colors at some point. I couldn't hide; there was no point in trying. The whole idea of the trip was to assess if we could be together 24 hours a day, seven days a week. We knew that there would be stressful times; we'd have to be each other's best friend to pull through. *Qué sera, sera* I sang to myself as if comforted by my mother, the person I missed the most.

News came that my father was already looking forward to November; he was anxious to see the whole family come together for Danny and Annamaria's wedding on the 14th. That Geoffrey was still doing well and would be attending the ceremony was a big plus. Family pictures were sure to be taken.

33

Burgers and Chablis

As much as I hated winter (and still do), I watched figure skating on television at every opportunity; Skate Canada, Skate America, the Canadian Nationals, the American Nationals, the NHK Cup to name a few. Over the years, I admired many of the world's great skaters but my heart belonged to our incredible Canadian athletes including Barbara-Ann Scott, Karen Magnussen, Toller Cranston, Brian Orser, Kurt Browning and Elizabeth Manley, among others. In the early 1970s, after overcoming stress fractures in both legs, Karen Magnussen placed 2nd in the 1972 Olympics and won the 1973 world title. In 1986, an emerging Kurt Browning was making waves in the figure skating community; he was destined to become a world-class competitor. Tall and handsome, Kurt was about to land the first quadruple in competition and wow the world.

Thanks to former Governor General Lord Minto, the Minto prizes for figure skating started in 1903, encouraging many young boys and girls to excel in this emerging sport. As far back as I can remember, I was hooked on ice skating. I could not have been more than 10 years old when I saw figure skating for the first time at the Dalhousie Arena. In those days, most boys would have not considered figure skating; boys played hockey and girls figure skated. Watching the Canadian Nationals in 1986, I no longer had to hide my passion for this sport. Lord Minto had been quite the visionary; he had wanted *to encourage the development of skillful performance in figures.* His goal has certainly been achieved; I was a witness to the talent produced in this country and was proud that Canada dominated this sport for many years.

On a regular basis, Norman and I would meet and have dinner. It had been ten years since I had arrived in Ottawa; I had Norman to thank for all the help he had given me to settle in this new cosmopolitan city. Invariably, we talked about our early years in Ottawa; it wasn't always easy to meet new people and bars weren't the best place to seek new friendships.

'Do you remember the *Friday night group*?' I said.

'Oh yes, I do,' replied Norman. 'You asked me to join you a few times. If I remember correctly, the location of meetings rotated from one place to the next depending on who wanted to host. I went twice when the group met on Stewart Street.'

'Do you recall an early October evening when the group was discussing plans for a Halloween party?' I asked.

'Yes, yes, yes, I remember that we were a large group which included an Anglican minister and Paul Lajoie, an out-of-costume drag queen by the name of Coco Paradise who went unnoticed by most people in the room,' added Norman.

'That was quite the night,' I replied.

The discussion about that Halloween party got quite lively as many did not see the point of dressing up. Paul Lajoie was making suggestions as to appropriate costumes for each person. When he got to the Anglican Minister who had been quite vocal in his opposition to the requirement to come in costume, Paul (a.k.a. Coco Paradise) looked at him straight in the eye and said: '*Oh, just shove a raisin up your arse and come as a muffin!*' The room fell silent.

'Coco certainly had a way with words,' said Norman.

'You're no shrinking violet when it comes to making a point either,' I said. 'Don't you remember what you said to that old balding woman who came in to have her hair done and wanted to look like Farrah Fawcett-Majors?' I said.

Norman blushed. How could he ever forget what he had said to this tired old lady whose face was wrinkled from way too much sun and whose balding head had seen too many bleach jobs and perms, *Ma'am, for miracles, you'll have to go across the street to the Cathedral!*

Whenever I was feeling low and needed a quick boost, I'd call Norman and in no time he would have me in stitches. His brand of humor and his recall of details of stories long past was phenomenal. Everyone forgave him for his predilection for slight exaggerations to make a story even funnier.

A window opened for me in June of 1986. It was an important turning point, one that would mark the rest of my working life. Almost out of the blue, I was offered an opportunity to work in the Human Resources Sector of Energy, Mines and Resources Canada. My big break came as a result of an urgent need to fill a position in the Human Resources Planning Division under the guidance of Peter Gendron. I had heard that he was looking to fill a vacancy; I had the gall to approach him and tell him that I was the person he was looking for. I did this knowing that I had no experience in human resources planning and that none of my background supported my proposal. This unexpected career move gave me a huge confidence boost, as I was able to demonstrate within six months that the right choice had been made. What was initially a temporary assignment turned into a permanent move complete with change of job classification.

A few weeks later at a dinner party hosted by Dick Howard, a friend of Norman, I learned of a new employment trend in the gay community. Dick and his then partner Shamus had hired Frankie Bouchez one of the many young gay men who did house cleaning in the nude. I couldn't see the point of this. In our cold climate, working in the buff would mean raising the thermostat to ensure the comfort of the maid: an expensive proposition to say the least. As Norman had pointed out, other than having a place to hang your rag, there were few benefits to doing house work in one's birthday suit!

My social calendar was chock-a-block with dinner parties, garden parties, outings to craft shows and antique shows, and to the National Arts Centre. During the summer months, one could expect to be invited to several garden parties. One well-known couple in Ottawa was Bill and Bruce, a.k.a. Mutt and Jeff. Not only were they very different in height, they had very divergent tastes. Every summer, they hosted a garden party called 'Hot dogs and beer or Burgers and Chablis'. It was as if they were catering to two different groups; Bruce was a hot dog and beer kind of guy, while Bill, a more refined person, was definitely a burger and Chablis type. As an alternative to meeting new people in bars or in private discussion groups, these parties were, in my opinion, a wonderful way to be with friends and meet new people. There were many such social circles in Ottawa; in each, you would find some people you knew well and new faces that were either visitors to our town or people that you simply had not yet met.

While on assignment in Ottawa for three months, my sister Claire moved in for an eight-month period. The guest bedroom which had rarely been occupied was being put to good use. I enjoyed Claire's company; her *joie de vivre* was contagious. It gave her a good opportunity to get to know Jonathan; they took to each other rather well, as I had expected.

By the end of August, I was itching to go to Provincetown; this time Jonathan would be coming along. Michael was now seeing a new guy by the name of Joey and they had decided to be in Provincetown at the same time we would be there. They rented a small chalet on Cottage Street right behind Tillie's Cottages on Bradford Street. As usual during our stay, we ate lobster rolls at the Dairy Queen, went to the tea dance at the Boatslip almost every day, took a day trip to Nantucket, and walked Commercial Street from one end to the other every night. One of the guys in unit # 3 went fishing on the pier and brought back half a dozen fish which he gave us because he didn't eat anything that lived in water. Baked, the monk fish was very good; Jonathan and I had a delicious, completely unexpected feast.

For the first time in my life, I chose not to spend Christmas with my family in Dalhousie. Going back to 626 Victoria Street, the house where my mother had been omnipresent, was so painful that I preferred staying away. Not that I needed any excuse, but I wanted to spend Christmas in Ottawa with Jonathan; he had increasingly become a significant part of my life and I did not want to leave him behind.

34

The Journey Begins

In the days leading up to our trip to Europe in September 1991, I started wondering if I had made the right decision; this make-or-break holiday would reveal much about each person. Would I find out new things about Joshua that I hadn't suspected? Would any revelations about his character lead to a break-up?

If Joshua had any misgivings about the journey, he didn't share them with me. He was upbeat; his smile said a lot about his eagerness to get on with this one-time adventure. Although he had been to Europe as a teenager, he had never gone back. Much of what we had planned to see would be uncharted territory; the main exception was Venice.

Going to Europe for the first time at the age of 40, I wanted this holiday to be memorable for the right reasons. Not knowing what to expect was at once frightening and a saving grace. We had meticulously planned our itinerary with enough flexibility to spend extra time in any one place if we felt we wanted to see more.

Our decision to rent a car and tour on our own would give us the flexibility to travel at a more relaxed pace than a bus tour. We wanted to have the ability to take old country roads, to visit small villages that were off the beaten track and had fewer tourists.

The Ottawa-Amsterdam flight arrived on time at Schiphol Airport at 9am. I gasped at the size of the facility; so many runways, so many airlines that I had never heard of before, and so many stores in the terminal. With people from the four corners of the world, coming and going in all directions with endless moving walkways, it felt like we had entered the tower of Babel. With safety our primary concern in such a huge airport, we stayed together at all times, even going to the washroom together so that we wouldn't lose sight of one another.

Our first goal was to find the car rental office. Thank God for English-language signage clearly indicating the way; we found the pick up area where people were loaded into vans and brought to the appropriate car leasing agencies. Within minutes of checking in, we were on our way to the city.

Guessing that it might be difficult to get a decent room in Amsterdam, we had pre-booked a five night stay at the New York Hotel on Herengratch advertised in several gay directories. In keeping with most buildings in the core of Amsterdam, our hotel was quite narrow with only four stories. Built around a small square terrace, our inside room looked out onto the patio below and faced other rooms which seemed about 10 feet away from ours. When we looked out, we saw several guys sitting on window ledges; at first we weren't sure if they were just taking in fresh air or if they were 'rent' boys.

The innkeeper was French; he was very helpful in getting us safely parked in a tiny space in the garage. Réjean gave us a quick rundown of the surrounding area telling us what to see and what to avoid. With city maps in hand, we spent the day roaming along the beautiful canals of the Garden District. We hadn't anticipated warm weather but on this 28th day of September, the thermometer hit 24 degrees Celsius, warm enough to wear shorts. We had left them at home.

One of our objectives on our second day in Holland was to buy train tickets to Zoetermeer to see the *Floriade* (floral show); 70 hectares of plants, flowers, trees and shrubs. Our hotel was within walking distance of the Amsterdam Central Railway Station which made it convenient to purchase our tickets to the show. On approaching the station, we noticed a number of young people milling around; some were obviously trying to sell their wares (drugs of all kinds) to passersby. We walked briskly to avoid the drug pushers; our strategy worked well.

In a mostly commercial section of the city, we came across the Amsterdam Sexmuseum; we had no prior knowledge of this place at 18 Damrak Street. Joshua insisted that we go in; I think the word 'museum' sold him on the idea that he would be seeing a well documented exhibit. It wasn't what he expected, but it sure gave us lots of giggles. It was time well spent on a miserable rainy evening.

On our way back to our room, we walked along the same pedestrian street we had taken earlier. The businesses had closed for the night. As we would later learn, due to vandalism, store owners cover up their windows when the business is closed. Sheets of grey metal are pulled down like window blinds which are used as canvases by graffiti artists. A long street of high-end boutiques was turned into a graveyard looking alley which scared us, as there were few exits along this curved outdoor shopping concourse. It didn't help that the few people milling about looked stoned or were selling drugs; we were afraid that our North American looks would get us into trouble. Fortunately, we got back to our hotel safely and avoided that street at night afterwards.

There were two museums Joshua and I wanted to see: the Rijksmuseum and the Van Gogh Museum. At the Rijks, our main interests were the works of Rembrandt, Michelangelo, Rubens, and Vermeer. We were stunned by the colors and lighting in the Rembrandt paintings. Although most of his works are dark and somber, the intensity of the light and the attention to detail are breathtaking. Difficult to imagine that the paintings were made in the 1600s; he lived from 1606 to 1669.

Close to the Magna Plaza, we found stores selling CDs where Joshua had a field day; there was so much music available that never reached the North American shores. We spent considerable time in stores such as Fame and Virgin. Joshua couldn't resist the temptation to buy what he knew was not available in Canada. If the purchases were too numerous, he had the option to mail them back to Canada.

Our hotel was close to the famous Anne Frank House on Prinsengratch. The house is now a museum dedicated to the Jewish wartime diarist who, with her family and four other people, avoided persecution in hidden rooms at the rear of the building. Behind a bookcase that covered the entrance to the 'Secret Annex', Anne spent 25 months in hiding during which time she recorded in a diary the description of the hideout as well as the events that filled their days. It is a very touching memorial; at the end of the tour, Joshua and I left in silence as though we had been taught a very powerful lesson in persecution and discrimination, things we thought we knew much about.

In sharp contrast, we walked the red light district: a must for first-time visitors to Amsterdam. The girls dressed in the skimpiest apparel sit in showcase windows smiling at passersby to try to get their attention. Customers, with credit card in hand, pay for the transaction beforehand and the red curtain is then drawn indicating that the lady of the night is temporarily unavailable.

On our way back to our hotel, we were offered cocaine; we were not interested and we did not enquire about the price. What was surprising was the availability of this drug and the number of people out on the street selling it. At specialized government-authorized establishments, usually coffee shops, marijuana was bought and consumed on location. It was evident that many people had graduated to hard drugs, and later turned to the streets to sell the illicit stuff to make money to buy more of their preferred substances. After dark, Amsterdam gets a bit scary as drug pushers take over the streets approaching as many people as they can.

Before we got to the New York Hotel, we saw a small bookstore that looked interesting. Once inside, we looked around and noticed a stairwell that led to something called the Blue Boy. We looked at each other and one of us said 'nightcap?' and up we went. It wasn't very late; we expected that the bar would be almost empty. There were about a dozen people including the bartenders. We sat on stools at the bar right next to a gentleman who was also Canadian. We ordered beer. It took us a bit of time to realize that we were in a male brothel. One of the bartenders enquired whether we had made a selection. Confused about his question, the man sitting next to us explained that apart from the three of us, anyone of the other men were available for sex in closed rooms at the back of the bar. We explained that we had just come in for a beer; that response drew a half smile from the bartender. About 20 minutes later, a large three-ring binder was placed in front us; the bartender explained that he could get anyone of the men pictured in the album to come in within 10 to 15 minutes. All we had to do was to give him our order. Another staircase on the opposite side of the building led to a coffee shop on the lower level. As we entered the room, many turned their head to look at us. They must have thought we had bought services from the guys upstairs; we quickly left through the front door laughing as we walked in the direction of our hotel.

Our evening of adventure was not quite over. The rooms in the New York Hotel have windows that face tiny inner courtyards. Joshua opened the curtain to find men in other rooms sitting on the windowsills waiting for invitations. Just across our room on the next level was a nice-looking man wearing only the bare essentials trying his best to get Joshua's attention. The attractive-looking man was obviously on the prowl; the sheen on his body looked like he had rubbed oil on his skin to make it gleam. Gently, he caressed his torso spending a lot of time playing with his nipples. The seductive motions were meant to encourage Joshua to reciprocate. I took one look at this guy and I knew what he wanted.

'Close that curtain and come to bed, please,' I pleaded.

'Did you know about this place when you booked?' asked Joshua.

'No!' I replied. 'But I'm not sure I would have avoided this place because of it. The hotel is very affordable, has on-site parking which is rare in Amsterdam and includes continental breakfast.'

'Let's get some sleep,' said Joshua. 'I'm sure this guy will find a mate before the night is over.'

After all, this was Amsterdam; we knew that just about anything goes. We weren't going to let this get in the way of our having a great time in Holland. It was amusing to watch; we would probably never see this again. And so, the real European journey began!

35

Another Relationship Tethers

In late summer of 1986, I felt the lure of Provincetown again. There was no escaping it. Using colorful descriptions of this small Portuguese fishing village turned gay resort, I convinced Jonathan to make the trip with me. Although he had traveled extensively, he had not been to a gay resort town. He had been to far away places such as Berlin and Moscow but had never been to Cape Cod. If the beautiful men that flock to this coastal community every year didn't interest him, then the salty air and the seascapes would certainly grab his attention.

The drive to Cape Cod from Ottawa took, on average, 12 hours, particularly when going through Boston, which is what we did. We purposely chose to stop and spend some time in the Tea Party city as Jonathan had never been. We visited historic Faneuil Hall Marketplace within a stone's throw from the waterfront. A gift to the city by Peter Faneuil and opened in 1742, the brick marketplace building was rebuilt several times over the years. The current red brick building stands proudly as the 'cradle of liberty'.

The next morning, we discovered that the car locks had been picked and needed to be changed before we could continue on our journey. The word 'liberty' certainly didn't mean that someone could help themselves to our belongings. We were relieved that the pranksters had probably been caught in the act as nothing was missing. Or perhaps, they had found the canned goods, dish soap and paper towels, and decided that there was no point in taking worthless items. Nothing in the car would be suitable for a pawn shop.

We reached Provincetown on a sunny Saturday morning. We avoided the usual congestion on Route 6A by arriving early in the day before the Boston crowd made it to P-Town and in time for the tea dance. Salt box houses built on sandy lots lined the long road from the Sagamore Bridge to the end of 6A at the tip of Cape Cod in P-Town. The further up you drove, the narrower the peninsula and the smaller the trees.

It was exciting for me to be going there with Jonathan. He would certainly enjoy the sights, and the gay men would certainly enjoy looking at him. With his boyish good looks, akin to Tintin, he would draw attention from many of the guys walking along Commercial Street.

Provincetown is very much a seaside resort with an abundance of exotic and often expensive seasonal properties. There are no tall buildings. Most constructions are wood; buildings are clad in shingles left unpainted which turn grey over time. White is the dominant color used to accent the grey colored Cape Cod Colonial homes which come in a variety of shapes and sizes. Many of the older homes have been lovingly restored by gay men who have turned them into elegant B&Bs. Some of these include the White Wood Inn, Admiral's Landing, Christopher's by the Bay and Gifford House, to name a few.

Restaurants come and go but a few have been around for as long as I can remember. Places such as Vorelli's, Central Station, the Lobster Pot and the Front Street Restaurant are iconic. Spiritus Pizza has had a long tradition of serving pizza at all hours of the day and night. It's legendary!

It was while we were in Cape Cod that I became aware that my relationship with Jonathan wasn't going in the direction that I had hoped. There were no fights, no embarrassing moments, and no disagreements; simply, we weren't gelling. I had hoped that the trip to Provincetown would be good for us as he would see many other happy couples. Surely positive images of long-term relationships would have an encouraging effect on him. Some days, I wasn't sure if he wanted to be with me or if he was ready to move on, but I couldn't come to terms with the let-down that would necessarily follow a break-up. I conveniently ignored the feelings I was having and focused on the fun things we did. His independent streak would eventually come to the fore in due time. Now was not the time to force the issue.

Along with two friends from Ottawa also in Provincetown at the same time, we decided to take a side trip to Nantucket. This pleasant one-day excursion was a success. All of us enjoyed the ferry ride from the mainland to the island. As we walked Main Street and Broad Street, we admired the well-kept properties, the old style architecture and the tall trees. Everything was perfect. Almost *disney-esque*! We shopped, snapped a few pictures and sat down to eat a quick meal before walking back to the wharf for the return trip. There was contentment in Jonathan's eyes but it had nothing to do with us as a couple.

Back in Ottawa, things returned to normal. Our routine consisted of weekend visits only. Jonathan shared an apartment with a close friend. Although I suspected that they had had a relationship at one time, I was not about to poke my nose into his affairs. There was never any talk about him moving in with me; as much as he liked the art deco elements of my apartment, he certainly wasn't making any overtures to me about living together. My analysis of our situation led me to believe that perhaps his Germanic ancestry prevented him from showing much affection. Macho men find it difficult to say "I love you". I did not expect him to say it to me but I was hoping that he would find other ways of letting me know his feelings. He never did, and I never found out where I stood with him.

We continued to do things together on weekends. We took a trip to Montréal to visit one of my friends and to do some shopping. As long as I didn't get into touchy-feely subjects, we were fine. Not wanting to rile him up, I avoided any topic of conversation that I knew would lead to confrontation. He was not a difficult person; he was meek and mild. Rather than face conflict, he walked away. Not open to long discussions about him, I was not able to really find out who he was, what mattered to him. I felt his unhappiness. He lad lost his father when he was young boy. Maybe the blow of that unfortunate passing had a more profound impact than he himself could fathom.

I still treasure the gifts he gave me for Christmas that year. Deep down, I still love him dearly. His love of all things beautiful had led him to purchase a beautiful glass egg in various shades of mustard yellow. The symbolism of the egg (the beginning of life) was not lost on me. Did Jonathan make that connection when he bought this item? Was he telling me that a new beginning was just around the corner? That it was yellow was not accident as it was one of his favorite colors. I have always taken extra precaution to ensure that this treasured keepsake, one of my most valuable possessions, is well guarded. It serves as a link to my relationship with a person who meant a lot me. Unrequited love is often the hardest kind.

Jonathan and I attended Norman and Leon's New Year's Levee. Leon was of the opinion that if the Governor General could host a huge levee, so could he. That year more than 100 people had come during the eight hour open house event. Leon's traditional Christmas baking was everywhere, served in every room on the main level of their home at 222 Armstrong Street. Most of the people attending were either friends of Leon through Club Moustache, a like-minded group of gay men involved in all types of sporting events, or Norman's numerous followers which included the 15 to 20 guys of the Stitch and Bitch Club. These guys met on a semi-monthly basis to work on knitting, sewing or needlework projects while they shot the breeze about what was happening, or not, in Ottawa.

Some of the guys were obviously going through difficult times. They were unwell. Many of their friends had already passed away because of AIDS. More would follow. At this party, I could easily identify four or five who were on their way out. It pained me. I worried that Jonathan would be afraid of a relationship with me because so many of my circle of friends were disappearing at an alarming rate. There was no point in trying to reassure him. I had been as promiscuous as the next person and I couldn't expect to be spared. Jonathan and I had never been comfortable with each other sexually. I wondered if the AIDS crisis made it difficult for him to feel comfortable with me. I didn't expect him to let his guard down, but was hopeful that he would at least find a modicum of happiness in our relationship.

36

The First Leg

Our month-long European exploration in the fall of 1991 continued from Amsterdam as we drove south to Maastricht on our way to Germany. We knew very little about this charming town before we decided to stop for food and much needed rest. We had not read up about it before leaving home. Better known because of the Treaty on European Union signed on February 7th 1992, this Dutch town on the banks of the Meuse River is the capital of the province of Limburg. This former Roman settlement prides itself in having an ancient Roman bridge with beautiful arches and the stunning Basilica of Saint Servatius.

I hadn't planned on being the head chauffeur but it quickly became clear to me that Joshua would not be able to handle the stress of driving in a foreign land. I happily took this responsibility as I knew he would prove to be an excellent co-pilot. Over the course of our trip, he admitted that he has a fear of heights; driving on elevated highways or over long waterways was something he did not wish to do.

Our objective for the first day on the road was to reach Köln (Cologne). As the fourth largest German city after Berlin, Hamburg and Munich, Köln was founded and established in the first century AD. One of the most heavily bombed cities in Germany during World War II, it was almost entirely destroyed; thus the rebuilding which has resulted in a very mixed and unique cityscape.

The Kölner Dom (Cologne Cathedral) dominates the city. We walked around it to admire its incredible gothic structure. Construction commenced in 1248 and was not completed until 1880; the cathedral boasts the largest façade of any church in the world. From there, we happened upon a huge outdoor antique and flea market. By now, Joshua had developed a keen interest in such markets; we spent some time checking out the unusual merchandize; things we don't see in North America.

While wandering in the market, we noticed many people with severe deformities, a much higher percentage than would be expected in the general population. Without saying anything to each other, we thought it odd that so many unusual individuals would find themselves in the same place. None of them were vendors; all were milling around without any obvious interest in the articles for sale.

'I think we should move on,' I said to Joshua.

'Not a bad idea,' he quickly replied. 'It's not that I feel unsafe but this place seems strange.'

'Let's walk around a bit more before we go back to our room', I suggested.

'Wonder if we could find a gay bar?' Joshua enquired.

The historic part of the city (zentrum) with swank hotels and neat cafés was almost deserted so we decided to walk towards our hotel which was in the gay ghetto. There we found a 'wrinkle' bar filled with more strange looking men staring at us. After a quick drink, we headed for our hotel for a good night's rest.

'Is it me or is this place a bit creepy?' I asked.

'Can't say that I felt comfortable in the places we checked out this evening,' said Josh. 'Maybe we are just too tired to enjoy the sights. It will all look very different in the morning. Let's not rush to judgment.'

I was feeling a bit let down that night; I kept my feelings to myself and Joshua did the same. Neither of us was relaxed in this peculiar German city of which we knew very little. We had been told that Germans are not particularly friendly to outsiders; our expectations weren't high but we did not anticipate this feeling of alienation. Had the accumulated fatigue of the first five days of travel started to affect our spirits?

Joshua fell asleep very quickly, almost the very minute that his head hit the pillow. It was quite a different story for me; my mind was racing and sleep would not come. I worried that we would have more difficult days like this one. With a bit of luck the next destination would be uplifting and the gloom forgotten.

37

A Season of Losses

My sister's time in Ottawa in 1987 helped me get through a difficult and dark period of my life. AIDS was affecting many of my friends; sadness overtook me most days. My relationship with Jonathan was getting weaker and I knew it was only a matter of time before he would walk away. By Easter, Claire had ended her project and was back in Halifax. In early July, without any warning or explanation, Jonathan simply stopped calling. It wasn't a total surprise. As with any breakup, I was devastated; my heart sunk as low at it could go. I felt rejected!

It took time for me to heal; I needed to feel good about myself again. However, that was a tall order. Why should I feel good about myself when so many around me were suffering? Catholics are raised on principles of guilt and I was no exception. I felt guilty for being relatively healthy. I also felt excluded for being successful. In the end, I felt I didn't belong, an outcast with very few close friends.

My heart went out to Norman my bosom buddy who at this point was in the 'full blown AIDS' stage. His mother Mea had moved to Ottawa to be closer to him and to take care of him. His bout with shingles left me speechless; the rash followed a straight line from his back to his abdomen, up to his face and across the right eye. Mega doses of morphine did little to ease the pain. How could this happen? A person so caring and so gentle was being ferociously attacked when his natural defenses were at their weakest! How could a loving God allow such misery? Hardly a day went by that I didn't seriously question my faith.

Had it not been for his Mom who cared for him on a daily basis, it would have been disastrous. Leon, who at that point knew that he was also HIV positive was getting weaker but not to the point that he couldn't help. He did all he could to see that Norman was treated with compassion by the myriad of helpers who came by every day. Norman's heath went from bad to worse; his mother moved in with them in their house at 222 Armstrong Street.

Word got around about this living arrangement; many others who were failing showed up for help and kind words. Mea always had time for anyone who needed her help. She had become a den mother to the Ottawa gay community. People were drawn to her like a magnet. She was a nun without uniform, an un-anointed saint! Little did she know what she would be getting herself into.

When things got too heavy for me, I arranged short trips. I decided to make the annual pilgrimage to Provincetown even though I would be alone for the duration. The week went by fast; there was nothing memorable during my time in P-Town. The return trip proved to be the best part of the holiday. I drove to Newport, Rhode Island to visit the mansions.

During the 19th century, wealthy southern plantation owners seeking to escape the heat began to build summer cottages on Bellevue Avenue such as Kingscote. Later, wealthy Yankees such as the Wetmore family also began constructing larger mansions such as Chateau-sur-Mer. Most of these early families made a substantial part of their fortunes in the Old China Trade. By the turn of the 20th century, many of the nation's wealthiest families (Vanderbilts, Astors, and Wideners) had large properties in Newport. They resided for a brief social season in grand, gilded mansions with elaborate receiving, dining, music and ballrooms, but with few bedrooms, since the guests were expected to have their own "cottages". Many of the homes were designed by the New York architect Richard Morris Hunt.

It was a real treat to visit all of the open mansions while I was there. The sad part is that I had nobody with whom to share this exciting excursion. For the would-be interior designer, this was a wonderful field trip; one that is often recommended to people who enjoy exquisite homes.

From Newport, I drove back to Ottawa stopping for short visits in New Haven and Hartford. I had hoped to see Justin and Shelley in Wallingford but as they had no idea I was passing through, neither could be found. It had been my mistake not to tell them that I was coming; the itinerary was planned one day at a time.

No sooner had I arrived in Ottawa that I received news that Norman was frail and may not last until Christmas. Leon and Mea had done all they could to make him comfortable. They were eager for me to come and see him while he was still able to talk for short periods of time. My last visit with Norman was difficult; words would not come to me. He knew me well enough to understand that although words had always been my passion, in hard times, I could easily become speechless. We spoke to each other with our eyes only. My love for him would continue long after his passing. He died on December 1st which ironically, a few years later, was proclaimed World AIDS Day.

A few weeks later, part of the Steeves clan was in Ottawa for Christmas which helped uplift my spirits. Family can be so supportive in time of need; the Steeves were no exception. The gift exchange on Christmas morning was a particularly touching moment for me. Congregated in my apartment were my father, my brothers Phil and Danny and my sister Claire. Phil's wife and two daughters were also present. Suzie, my neighbor from across the hall was in India for the holidays; she had given us access to her apartment so that everyone would have a bed in which to sleep. Our back-to-back kitchens opened to a fire escape stairwell which served as a conduit from one unit to the other. Meals were made, dishes were washed and dried. We laughed, talked, drank and walked in the freshly fallen snow. After they had left, I was struck with how well things often fall into place at the right time. I had needed my family and they were there. That special Christmas gathering was never repeated; maybe there was no need for it.

38

More of Germany

On October 3rd, we happily left Köln behind us and headed for Heidelberg in the hope of seeing the famous castle where the "The Student Prince" was filmed. Out of breath after climbing the 309 stairs, we were rewarded with stunning views of the castle and the baroque style old town below. It was a perfect antithesis to the previous day. Joshua was all smiles as he observed the details of the imposing structure. To think that this castle was partially rebuilt after its destruction in the 17th and 18th century added to its mystique. We strolled among the ruins of the castle some 154 years after French author Victor Hugo had done the very same thing.

Our next destination was Stuttgart which is surprisingly spread over several hills (many of them vineyards). Located in southern Germany and one hour from the Black Forest, the capital of the state of Baden-Württemberg has over 5 million inhabitants in its metropolitan area. "Stuttgart offers more" as the tourism slogan states.

Before leaving Ottawa, we had booked rooms in some of the larger cities we would be visiting for sure. We had no reservations for Stuttgart, however we drove as near the "centrum" as we could and located a small, clean hotel. There were no double rooms available, but they offered us two single rooms (with narrow single beds) for the same price. Since we were planning to spend just one night in the city, we agreed to the offer. The hotel appeared to be new; the rooms were tiny but very functional, reminiscent of cabins on a cruise ship.

We explored the city on foot; to our surprise, our accommodations were across from the main train station. Buildings were recent with a smattering of historic structures. It was obvious that the city had been badly damaged during the Second World War. The mall closest to our hotel was alive with people elegantly dressed; they were going to an evening theatre or opera performance. Slowly, we made our way back to our hotel all the while taking in as much as our eyes could handle. Everywhere we looked, everything was clean and organized, as we had come to expect from the Germans. Tastefully decorated window displays showed the best of what could be bought. Most merchandise was German made.

The idea of separate quarters for the night, although acceptable for a short stay, was not my idea of a good time. Like school kids comparing their lunches, we visited each other's room only to find them almost identical; my room was slightly larger. What was really unusual was the fact that there were no windows in the rooms. On the back wall, a curtain with a light behind it gave the impression of a window; it was similar to the designs used for inside cabins on cruise ships. It had been years since I had slept in a single bed; it was a restless night.

I missed sharing my bed with Joshua; this was the first time we were together without sharing a room. It did not feel right; I was out of my comfort zone in more ways than one. Without realizing it, he offered a certain degree of protection. At breakfast the next morning, we shared our experiences; Joshua had fallen asleep quickly and had not felt any different by being alone in his room. He was and still is an independent type. I had noticed this before but this was a further confirmation.

Whizzing by on the autobahn at 140 to 160 kilometers were BMWs and Mercedes Benzs; our 4 cylinder sub-compact (can of sardines) could hardly keep pace. When the headlights of the car behind us were blinking, the message was that we were driving too slowly, even though we were in the right lane. I was the dedicated driver leaving Josh with the responsibility of advising me on all matters related to getting to our destination and interpreting traffic signs. Never once did he volunteer to take over, even when my stress levels were noticeable.

We arrived at our next destination, München (Munich), just before lunch. Without much effort, we located Hotel Blauer Bock on Sebastiansplatz, our three-star refuge for the following three nights. An austere looking place with employees to match; the old matron was not pleased that we couldn't speak German. Joshua took an instant dislike to her. With my limited

German (a couple of greeting words), she was a tad friendlier with me. She seemed proud to tell me that they offered indoor parking for which we were most grateful.

The charm of old Munich is evident from the time you reach the *centrum*. Friends of ours had told us a little bit about the city and suggested that we should not miss Marienplatz which is the city centre from where one can reach the Kaufingerstrasse Mall. The Marienplatz is dominated by the New City Hall whose main tower contains the *Glockenspiel* attracting thousands of tourists every day. Joshua found it rather ironic that 'town hall' in German is *Rathaus* which he jokingly pronounced 'rat house'. Later, we stopped to visit the Theatinerkirche, an Italian high-Baroque style church dating back to 1663, which is the burial place of the Bavarian royal family. The attached monastery destroyed during the Second World War was completely rebuilt by 1973.

Quite by chance, we walked into a restaurant frequented by members of the gay community. Vilinus Café had a very bohemian feel to it; the atmosphere was relaxed and the crowd was rather young. It was a very comfortable environment; we enjoyed our meal so much that we lingered there for part of the afternoon. With no precise destination in mind, we walked the streets of Munich poking in and out of churches, department stores and impressive hotel lobbies. We got a bit nostalgic when we saw a Burger King restaurant, so in we went and had a light supper. Back on the street, we noticed several fine looking men; we decided to follow them to see where they were going. We ended up in a smart bar-restaurant called the 'Nil' and not the swanky gay bar as we had expected.

When entering the Blauer Bock Hotel, one needs to get the room key which is kept by the stern-faced matron. Joshua asked for our room key but because he didn't use the German word for key, she looked at him as though she didn't understand. Luckily, I remembered the word 'schüssel'; she half-smiled and gave me our key. Joshua was not amused.

Breakfast next morning was typical of most of the ones we had during our month-long holiday. The hotel offered boiled eggs, ham, smoked salmon, spicy meats, yogurt, cereal, granola, cheese, fruit, pastries, bread, jam, juice and coffee. Fried bacon and eggs are not European; nowhere did we see these served. The smorgasbord style breakfast appealed to us as we ate what we liked and in quantities sufficient to last us until lunch. In some places, we took away apples, oranges or bananas that we ate as snacks.

Of all the places and things to see and do in Munich, Joshua was intent on spending time in the Englisher Garten, a 3.7 square kilometer garden created by Sir Benjamin Thompson in 1789 which remains to this day one of the world's largest urban public parks. Informal landscape gardening was the preferred style in the mid-18th century England. There, in Munich, the 'Garten' with its 36 kilometers of footpaths and over 100 bridges offers to the people of Munich an oasis that is second to none in the world. Central Park in New York City pales in comparison.

If a person's likes and dislikes can be read by looking at someone's face, then Joshua was certainly a nature lover. In the 'Garten' his eyes lit up; he was taking it all in as if he needed to sponge up as much energy as he could to make it last. He was in a trance for the first half hour in the park. When he did finally speak, I learned that it was the informality of the landscape that impressed him the most. None of the French manicured gardens here; just tall trees, endless meadows and meandering brooks with a few interesting architectural structures such as the Japanese temple to create points of interest. Larger than New York's Central Park, the Englisher Garten is huge; a bicycle would have been ideal to see it all. Nevertheless, our three-hour walk gave us a good idea of this unique urban park.

At the World of Music store, Joshua found more CDs for his collection. We would have to figure out how we could bring back the stash of CDs; we had way too many to bring back in our luggage. On our way to the 'Nil' restaurant for our evening meal, Joshua mentioned that we should consider shipping a box of CDs to Ottawa. Walking back to the hotel, we planned the next day's outings. Both fond of architecture, we were eager to visit European castles and palaces particularly those that had been restored and furnished. Munich would not disappoint!

Under glorious sunshine and a temperature of 22 degrees Celsius, we set out to see the Nymphenberg Palace on the outskirts of Munich. Built on a 490 acre site, construction began in 1664; the Palace was the home of the Bavarian royal family and is the birthplace of King Ludwig II who had a lifelong friendship with Otto von Bismarck. The main building consists of the Central, Northern and Southern pavilions. An extra five pavilions dot the enormous property. The baroque facades comprise an overall width of about 700 meters. Over the years the palace has been modified: some rooms still show their original baroque decoration while others were later redesigned in rococo or neoclassical style. Our extended visit included a walk in the palace grounds; noticing that the Amalienburg (hunting lodge) pavilion was open, we took advantage of the opportunity. Once inside, we saw a German filming crew at work; they were taping a tourism video and asked if we wanted to be in it. Wholeheartedly we agreed to the non speaking roles; we did a few takes before being dismissed. We never did see the finished product.

Our stay in Munich coincided with Oktoberfest. The streets and outdoor pubs were filled with happy-faced men and women in traditional Bavarian clothing. Overweight and smiling male and female staff members each carrying 3 to 4 overflowing beer steins in each hand zipped along the rows of tables protected by hanging white awnings. For each of these pubs, there was live music, usually a three- or four-piece band playing traditional tunes. Between gulps of beer, people ate oversized pretzels sprinkled with salt. We were assigned seats at a long table with other partygoers; conversation was difficult but the drinking was easy. Although we weren't wearing *lederhosen*, we fit in with the crowd; Germans work hard but they also play hard. It was nice to see the leisure side of a strict and serious society.

Joshua was relieved to find that not every German was as stone-faced as the hotel matron. In this highly organized country where trains run on time and rules are diligently followed, we came to appreciate the hard-working men and women we dealt with at various locations. Inflexible as they first appear, they can be helpful and gracious; we had learned much about the German folk. There was a lot more to see and do here but we had to move on.

39

Ten Trips

My friends often referred to me as the 'world traveler'; in 1988 alone, I took ten trips. Exploring new places and experiencing different cultures had been engrained in me as a kid. Part of me enjoyed being away from the day-to-day grind; I always found it refreshing to take a few steps back and to return to my routine, rested with a renewed sense of purpose. It was a wonderful way to help me through difficult times; the past few years had taken their toll on me. When an opportunity to travel to Turkey came up, I was excited to think that I would visit a friend who was living half way across the globe.

One of the ladies at work had gone to Turkey on a holiday, and fell in love with the country (and with a Turk). Rita met Ian at a restaurant; it was love at first sight. He convinced her to move to Turkey to be with him. So desperate was she to find romance that this invitation was just too good to pass up. She requested and got approval to take a year off without pay; her job would be protected so that she could reintegrate her position upon her return, if she so chose.

While Rita was getting ready for the move, she convinced my colleague Carmen (who had also worked with Rita) and I to visit her and Ian in Istanbul. We would tour around with Ian and her. One of the trips would be to Ankara, the capital city. She had it under good authority that the Turkish government was keen on employing international consultants to perform a variety of tasks. Ian would bid on the work supported by a proposal that Rita, Carmen and I would hammer out. The idea was to find meaningful employment for Rita while giving Carmen and I international exposure. The trip to Ankara was to attend a bidder's conference.

For Carmen and I, this was our very first trip to a Muslim country. Rita had assured us that although the security guards at the Istanbul airport would have machine guns at the ready, we were not to be alarmed as this was how things were in Turkey. A strikingly attractive tall blonde, Carmen was sure to attract interest wherever we went; Rita had already experienced this first hand.

We were warmly greeted at the airport by Ian and Rita and were shown the main sights: the Blue Mosque, Topkapi Palace, the Spice Bazaar, the Grand Bazaar, the elegant hotels around Taksim Square and some fine restaurants. By the end of our first week there, we noticed that the relationship between Rita and Ian was not what we had expected. There was tension in the air at all times; Rita had brought her son to live with them which added to the stress levels. Ian spoke to Rita in a condescending way; he would raise his voice to make a point. Carmen suspected that Ian was physically abusive; there was talk about aborting the trip. I resisted Carmen's suggestion knowing that we would be severely offending our hosts, a mistake that could cost us dearly in the long run. After lengthy discussions, we opted to stay.

Our excursion to Ankara was quite the eye opener; on a two-lane highway congested with cars and trucks, passing another vehicle is achieved by having both the vehicle in front of you and the oncoming vehicle make room between them to allow for your safe passage. The first time this occurred, Carmen and I were as white as ghosts. Rita assured us that this was customary; rarely are there accidents because of it. It amazed us to see the goodwill of drivers accommodating each other in what we would have called a dare-devil approach to highway driving. As there were no passing lanes, high beams were used to signal a desire to overtake the car ahead. If nothing, these people were ingenious in the way they dealt with this less than ideal situation. At first, we were dumbfounded by what we believed to be necessary; there were no painted lines down the median; there was really no need for that kind of expense. Towards the end of the end of second week of our visit, we began to feel comfortable despite the huge cultural differences we were encountering.

Two rooms had been booked at the hotel; unmarried couples may not share a room. Ian and I were booked into one room while Rita and Carmen were assigned to a room on a different floor. In the elevator, room keys were traded; Ian was not about to share a room with me. I took no offense.

At the bidder's conference, conducted all in Turkish, Rita, Carmen and I were the only foreigners. There were very few women in the male-dominated room; I sensed that some of the officials wondered why we were there. Ian had focused on a request for proposal for work to be performed for the PTT (Turkish Post Office); some of the instructions given were helpful. We needed as much background material as we could get in order to draft a reasonable proposal.

Right after the meeting, we drove back to Istanbul and immediately got to work. A desktop computer borrowed from Ian's relatives made the task of developing the proposal a bit easier notwithstanding the fact that the Turkish keyboard gave us a hard time. All of the Easter weekend was consumed with the preparation of this document in the hope that it would give us a good chance at getting the contract. By this time, the relationship with our hosts had soured somewhat; in this second week, I was the one who wanted to terminate the jaunt. Carmen convinced me to hang on; if we played our cards right, we could get to the end of this miserable ordeal and fly back to Canada without creating a scene. Commonsense prevailed; but the last few days were touch and go.

On the plane that took us back to Montreal, Carmen and I talked at length about our Turkish experience. We wondered if we had been foolish to accept the invitation in the first place. In our opinion, the relationship between Ian and Rita would probably get worse; we feared for her safety. In the end, someone else was the successful bidder; we never heard from Rita again.

Not long after my return from Turkey, another office colleague with whom I shared many interests invited me to an antique show in Montreal. A few weeks later, along with my brother Phil and his wife Janice, I attended the Flamboro Antique Outdoor Show. In the twelve years since I had moved to Ottawa, my interest in antiques and nostalgia items grew from year to year. It was in Flamboro that I bought a platter and a bowl that would later lead me to collecting Depression-era glass.

Through my friend Michael, I met John Edwards at a dinner party; he was moving to Ottawa to take up a job at the main library of the University of Ottawa. John and I hit it off well. Tall, dark and handsome, he had boyish looks that made him appear mischievous. He was looking to rent a room until he found an apartment, and so I offered my second bedroom. On John's bucket list was a visit to Niagara Falls; I made it happen for him. We drove to Niagara-on-the-Lake where we had lunch and then on to Niagara Falls to see this extraordinary natural wonder. On our way back to Ottawa, we drove through Port Colborne, Kitchener and Toronto which allowed him to see more of Ontario.

My initial attraction to John died off rather quickly for reasons I still cannot explain. Possibly meeting a new person who impressed me a great deal had much to do with it. While cycling along Somerset Street, I met a cyclist by the name of Jim Chatsworth, a handsome, self-confident, bearded young man who showed considerable interest in me. He had just ended a long-term relationship; he was on the rebound. I was smitten by Jim, but not foolish enough not to know that the potential for a strong relationship was weak at best. We saw each other only on weekends; at least once a month, he went to visit family in southern Ontario. In October he announced that he had accepted a job offer in Toronto; he would be moving there before Christmas. Another relationship had just fizzled out! It wasn't meant to be so I moved on without too much pain, at least that's what I thought.

Early in 1989, my boss noticed that I was depressed. She suggested a trip to Montreal; I took her advice and booked a room at Le Chasseur, a gay B&B in the village. It helped me get over Jonathan and John. The similarity of their names had struck me as being odd. They were Virgos; so am I. How did I expect to have a good relationship with someone of the same zodiac sign? Almost every reference I read pointed to a tough time when two nit-picking Virgos expect to make a relationship work. A string of Virgos (Jim, John and a few others) had come into my life and while I seem to be attracted by men of the same zodiac sign as myself, experience had shown that it wasn't working for me. Oddly, both Virgos and Geminis are ruled by Mercury and ironically both Jean and Josh are born under this sign. A good omen?

40

A Taste of Austria

A mere two hours out of Munich, Salzburg was on the horizon. However unplanned our trip had been up to that point, Salzburg was different. It had two main attractions for me: I wanted to see Mozart's birthplace almost as much as anything having to do with the filming of "The Sound of Music". The architecture of old town Salzburg gives it an atmosphere of elegance and class. This picture-perfect UNESCO World Heritage Site with its 150,000 inhabitants is spectacular. The old town is dominated by its baroque towers, churches and the massive Hohensalzburg Castle which sits high above (one of the largest medieval castles in Europe).

It's no wonder that the film studios chose this town as the site for the filming of one of Hollywood's most beloved movies. Amongst the many beautiful buildings is the oldest religious house in the German-speaking world. The Nonnberg Abbey, founded in 714, acquired international fame as result of "The Sound of Music". Maria Augusta Kutchera, later Maria von Trapp, a postulant in the abbey whose life was the basis for the movie, was an orphan at 17 when, in 1923, she chose to join the Benedictine order. Julie Andrews' portrayal of Maria is, in my books, the most memorable film casting ever. I was in love with Julie. Had I been heterosexual, I would have looked for a reasonable facsimile of this stunning English actress; no other woman in the world had her grace, her beauty, her voice and her talent. Her British accent is a plus.

In addition to the Nonnberg Abbey, actual film locations included St. Peter's Cemetery, Leopoldskron Palace, Hellbrunn Palace and Mirabell Gardens where Maria and the children sang 'Do-Re-Mi' while walking around a fountain. "Edelweiss", also written for the movie, was adopted by the people of Salzburg; it is not the traditional Austrian song it was purported to be. We chose not to take The Sound of Music Tour preferring instead to walk around to the various sites. Once satisfied that I had seen some of the major film locations of the movie, I was ready to explore Mozart's birthplace.

Joshua was far more interested in Mozart than in The Sound of Music. With the help of a city map, we located 9 Getreidegasse, the house in which Mozart was born and raised before moving to Vienna. This multi-storied building had nothing of the charm of an old house we expected to see. Disappointed, we continued walking in the old town where every second shop sells something associated with Mozart; chocolates being the main product on offer. This commercialization of Mozart was to be expected; one can't blame the good people of Salzburg for tapping into it. Tourism in this charming town is big business and the townsfolk take it seriously.

On our way again, by mid-afternoon we were in the centre of Vienna, a much different place from Salzburg: impatient drivers and cars double parked everywhere. Our first impression of Austria's capital was not very good; old and dirty, the city and its inhabitants could use a sprucing up we thought. St. Stephen's Cathedral and the pedestrian shopping district that surrounds it were the exception. Here the shops are modern and clean; the people are attractive, well dressed and prosperous. We made it in time for an impressive late-afternoon organ recital in St. Stephen's. Not only was the interior of the church remarkable, the organist delivered a short concert which included various styles of sacred and profane music to the delight of the huge crowd that had gathered. We felt privileged to be at right place at the right time.

As expected, Vienna is a busy place and having a pre-booked room had been a good idea or so we thought. In the early days of Internet, we had managed to find what we thought would be suitable accommodations in central Vienna. Without pictures, one had to rely on the words which did not necessarily accurately describe the business. Hotel Minu 3 was a disaster the likes of which put a fair amount of stress on our relationship, although not the kind to complain when things are different from what he expected, Joshua was not comfortable at this location. In fact, staff members were quite unfriendly to the point that we wondered if it would have been better to look for alternate accommodations. We did try. In the end, due to the difficulty of locating an affordable room in this metropolis, we endured what we still refer to as the absolute worst hotel in the world; the comments on Trip Advisor confirm it. Had that web site been available in 1992, we would certainly not have stayed there.

The décor was very somber; dark brown curtains, filthy dusty-rose rug, faded green corduroy fabric bedspread, an uninspiring three-seater sofa, a very old glass and chrome coffee table and the most horrendous chandelier hanging from a fourteen-foot ceiling. All light bulbs were of extremely low wattage; you simply could not see the room properly (perhaps that was a blessing in disguise). We clung to each other out of fear and out of anxiety in the worst bed we had ever slept in.

Quite by accident, we came upon an exhibition at the Hofburg Palace, the winter residence of the Habsburg Dynasty, rulers of the Astro-Hungarian Empire. The show called '100' included displays of ordinary items in lots of one hundred. In addition, there were atypical exhibits such as a young couple asleep in the nude in a glass cube, and a rail porter taking luggage from one location to another and back again to the original spot. The use of live mannequins in a museum was a first for us; we wondered if they enjoyed their work.

The summer residence of the Habsburg monarchs is the 1,441 room imperial Rococo residence known as Schönbrunn on the outskirts of Vienna on the banks of the Danube. With over 2 million visitors a year, this is by far Vienna's most popular tourist destination. All of the rooms open to the public have been lavishly restored and furnished with authentic period furniture. It was obvious to me that Joshua was enjoying this tour as much as I did: definitely something we had in common. We noted with interest that the palace had been used as well by Napoleon (much to our surprise).

I knew that Joshua would enjoy the palace grounds; he had taken great pleasure in exploring the Englisher Garten in Munich. Leisurely, we sauntered the palace green to get a closer look at the Neptune Fountain and the Gloriette (a tall wall of 11 arches supported by Doric columns - which serves as a war memorial) which are the main outdoor attractions in the sprawling English landscape complete with an Arboretum and botanical gardens.

Palaces, parks and pastries were our main interests in Europe. Joshua could be enticed by any one of these. I suggested that we head to the State Opera House to taste Sacher Torte, one of the most famous Viennese culinary specialties, always on offer at the State Opera Café. Jonathan had been to Austria before I met him, he swore by this authentic chocolate cake which was invented in 1832 in Vienna. Just the thought of it still makes my mouth water. We explored the public spaces of this incredible performing arts building which dates back to 1862 and whose most famous luminaries include Gustav Mahler and Herbert von Karajan.

A huge quantity of CDs had been stashed in the car away from prying eyes; Joshua was determined to ship them to Ottawa. He packed them neatly into a box and sealed it; the destination and return addresses were the same. Off we went to the local Austrian Post Office; a huge building with very high ceilings. Joshua approached the first open wicket and handed his parcel; the postal official looked at it with quizzical eyes. Speaking in German at top speed, he said something which we could not comprehend. When he realized that we had not understood a single word, he pointed to the two addresses and shook his head from left to right indicating that this was not possible. My very limited knowledge of German was of no value in this situation. After a few minutes of silence, the postal worker motioned us to follow him to another wicket to get the matter sorted out. We suspected that one of his colleagues could speak English and that we would be able to explain our dilemma.

The frown on the second official was very telling; he was having none of it. We figured that he thought we were trying to circumvent Canadian customs importation tariffs. Once he understood the reason that the return address was the same as the destination address, he relented. It was simply a way of ensuring that the parcel would not be returned to Austria as we had no fixed address in Vienna. Was he bending the rules to accommodate us? He affixed the correct postage after collecting the money we owed.

To get a feeling for how the Viennese live, we spent time on Neubaugasse a popular side street off Mariahilfer Strasse. We stopped for coffee and pastries at Café Ritter, a Viennese institution. European coffee is so much stronger than ours; it took a fair amount of cream and sugar to make it palatable. Pastries were a different story; just looking at them would make you salivate and gain weight. The choices and variety were endless; we were like kids in a candy store.

We weren't sure if our clothing or our looks gave us away; we were definitely tourists in a foreign country. Occasionally, gay men would smile at us realizing that we were a couple. This welcomed acknowledgement went a long way in offsetting the negative emotions concerning our terrible accommodations.

41

Toronto the Terrific

A surprisingly large number of gay people from Ottawa, dissatisfied with life in a government town where the sidewalks are rolled up at 9 pm, move to either Montreal or Toronto. I had witnessed this since my early days in the Capital. Larger cities do offer more but I was quite content to live at a slower and more civilized pace in a city with lots of green spaces. Thoughts of pulling roots and taking residence in either of those cities had as much appeal to me as living on Mars. Pleasant to visit, after a weekend of merriment, I was always happy to pack my bags and return to the comforts of small town Ottawa. My life here was complete, although in the first years I lived in this green city, it was not always possible for me to find everything I wanted. The occasional trip typically combined shopping, bar hopping and meeting friends who had left the nation's capital for greener pastures.

Nonetheless the lure of the big city was always present and when, in the winter of 1989, I learned of a temporary work assignment in Toronto, I made it known that I was interested but only if it was for a finite period. The Immigration and Refugee Board was looking for an experienced staffing officer for their Front Street location. Getting regional experience without having to commit to a permanent move was a godsend. The department agreed to provide a substantial living allowance which allowed me to rent a room in the city and to fly back to Ottawa once a month. The caveat was that I had to agree to stay till the end of the year. My home department saw this as a great learning opportunity. I would remain an employee of Energy, Mines and Resources and would be expected to resume my normal duties at the end of the assignment.

In early April, I flew to Toronto and took up my new duties. I reported to the HR Manager in Ottawa but worked under the direction of the Regional Manager (Larry Matterhorn), an affable gay man with sharp business sense. His no-nonsense approach appealed to my Virgo personality; we got along quite well.

I was able to rent a room in a condo at 25 Maitland in the heart of the gay village; a stone's throw from 'Trax', a denim and leather bar. My life centered on work and this gay bar; there, I met Ronnie, a tall lanky man from Milton, with whom I confided. Over a short period of time, we became good friends; he knew the Toronto scene and could tell me who or what to avoid. Ronnie was a well-known leather man who was as gentle as a cat. I could count on bumping into him when I went out to 'Trax'. He was *always* there.

The front room of 'Trax' had been a funeral parlor long before the gay bar opened. In it, a grand piano and a small stand-up bar filled the available space. Every weekday evening, there was live music; an energetic young gay man played the piano and got the old queens singing. It was very touching; many of these men had no family. They were at their happiest belting out show tunes with their friends. Some of the younger guys who like me enjoyed show tunes would wander in from the rear bar to watch the unplanned nightly performances. I caught myself singing along with the old geezers hoping none of them would take notice, or worse still, hear me singing off-key!

"Phantom" had just begun at the restored Pantages Theatre. The piano man at Trax knew all the songs and the lyrics of this Andrew Lloyd Webber musical. Before going to Toronto, I had made a special trip to see Phantom; I was becoming quite familiar with the soundtrack. The more I heard this music, the more I liked it. I convinced Ronnie to join me on my birthday for a special night out on the town which included a meal in the dining room of the Windsor Arms Hotel and tickets for Phantom. It was even better the second time around.

If there was one distinct advantage of a large city, it was the access to musical performances on any given night. I could have spent a fortune on shows. My preference for choral music found satisfaction in a festival called the Joy of Singing which brought to Toronto choirs and vocal groups from Canada and from many parts of world. A concert by the 'King Singers' of England in Roy Thompson Hall was the epitome of musical perfection. This acapella group of men had the most polished voices I have ever heard. My taste in music included other genres and during my time in Toronto, I saw Dionne Warwick and Shirley Bassey perform. Ronnie insisted that I see a live performance of the Rocky Horror Picture Show at the Bathurst Theatre; he was right about it, the show lived up to its promise of memorable music and outlandish scripts.

Provincetown beckoned again; Labor Day weekend on the Cape is intoxicating. I altered my usual travel plans by going first to New Brunswick to see my father in Dalhousie. From there, I drove to Fredericton for a short visit with my brother Danny and his family. Since I had never been to Ogunquit, Maine, and as it was on my way to Cape Cod, I spent some time in this smallish resort that caters to many communities including gay men. Ogunquit is more upscale than Provincetown but its affluence tends to push away the very crowd it tries to attract. With less gay establishments than P-town, there is less to do there; there is the Ogunquit Playhouse, a long-established summer theatre that offers quality performances during the short tourist season. We never did go to that theatre as tickets were sold out well in advance of the shows.

Driving down Highway 95, I entered the Greater Boston area; you either take the ring road or drive through the city. On a Saturday morning, there was far less traffic so I chose the shortest route (through the city center). I had read about a proposal to build a huge underground highway that would allow traffic to avoid the more congested parts of the city. It would take a long time to build. Over the years, I had learned to avoid going anywhere near downtown Boston as the stop and go traffic added an hour or two of traveling time.

Few places can offer the tranquility found in P-town; it was one of the reasons I went there religiously every year in the fall. The combination of the warm sun, cool breeze, clean sand dunes, good food and excellent entertainment was difficult to beat. On each visit, Tillie and Clarence Kacergis, the owners of the suites I stayed in, made kale soup as a special treat. It was Tillie's unique way of thanking us, the Canadians who, every season, rented rooms in their small motel.

Torontonians are blessed with having excellent access to travel deals and last minute sell-offs. In search for a real bargain somewhere warmer and less dreary than Toronto in

November, my tall order was met by Cubana Air. It was offering daily flights to Varadero, including a one-week stay at Villa Cuba for a pittance. Villa Cuba was owned by the Dupont family before they hastily left the island; the property was taken over by the Castro government who operated it as an all-inclusive three star tourist resort. Rooms in the large guest cottages were rented out individually. There was nothing fancy about the place. Meals served in a facility that reminded me of a university cafeteria in Fredericton were adequate. It was strange to be in a place where there were virtually no Americans. It was stranger still that Germans had discovered the beauties of Cuba; the Gaviota Hotel, next to Villa Cuba could easily have been mistaken as a small German resort.

Although I enjoyed Toronto, the city lacked green spaces. Concrete everywhere! It was stifling; in the summer heat, the place was like an oven. With Ronnie as my guide, I discovered the Toronto islands which I considered the Central Park of the city. Only accessible by ferry in the summer, this urban oasis allowed the city folk to swim in Lake Ontario and sunbathe on near pristine beaches.

At the end of my assignment, I was happy to be heading back home to Ottawa. Another episode of my life had ended and I was looking forward to whatever lay ahead.

42

Bridge of Sighs to Ponte Vecchio

Austrian highways are like speedways; to avoid accidents, one has to keep pace with the flow. We drove above the posted speed limits but so did everybody else. The further from Vienna we were, the less congested it became. Route A-2 which is a North-South axis veers East-West about two hours east of Graz. Gently sloping downwards, the highway offers panoramas that are simply intoxicating. The closer we came to the city of Graz, the more annoyed I became that we had not planned on stopping in this beautiful small city. Intent on reaching Venice by nightfall, we had to be content with long-distance views of this large urban area.

Just beyond Graz but before entering Italy, at the end of a very long slant where the posted speed limit was significantly reduced, we were caught by police. We were hardly the only ones caught in the dragnet; many others who had not seen the ghost car halfway down the bank had also been pulled over, and charged with a hefty fine that had to be paid in cash on the spot. With $200 less in our pockets, we moved on. We were not amused! This was definitely a cash cow for the Austrian government and a sad farewell to foreigners exiting the country.

As we entered Italy where almost everything is posted in Italian only, we were confounded by their unique toll roads. An unmanned ticket dispenser at the side of the road appeared not to be in use; all the other drivers were whizzing by so we did likewise. A little further down the road, we understood that the cost for the use of the toll road was based on where we entered; not having taken a ticket from the toll machine meant that we had no proof of where we connected with this motorway, and thus we would likely pay a fine or a hefty amount. For the second time in a day, our wallets suffered a shock. In heavy rain and dense fog, we eventually reached Padua, the closest we could get to Venice with a car.

Finding a decent place to stay in a foreign country when it's dark and raining proved to be a bit trying on our relationship. I could sense that Joshua was showing restraint. He tended not to speak whenever he was stressed. Padua at nightfall was not an easy place to get around. After several failed attempts to find a hotel with a vacancy, we decided to try our luck at the Sheraton; keeping in mind the awful room in Vienna, an upgrade to a better hotel was in order. Forking out $200 a night, we were given a room fit for royalty with a full marble bathroom.

We settled in the room and then went out for a bite to eat; Joshua wanted Italian-style pizza. On via San Marco, we found the only restaurant open at that time; pizza would have to wait, it wasn't on the menu. Joshua suggested veal; his flair for good choices influenced me to follow suit. We were not disappointed.

The Sheraton hotel allowed travelers visiting Venice to leave their cars in the secured parking lot. A shuttle bus dropped us off at the wharf where we boarded a 'vaporetto' (water taxi) to the Grand Canal. Joshua had been to Italy as a young boy and had visited Venice on a school trip. He was looking forward to seeing the floating city once more. He was expecting knee high water in Piazza San Marco where flooding is a regular occurrence; when that happens, city officials quickly install temporary elevated walkways so that people can get around.

The iconic St. Mark's Campanile is what most people remember of Venice; this square tower is the most recognizable Venetian landmark in this extremely crowded metropolitan area. Although cars and trucks may access some parts of the city, the main island is pedestrian only with access via the many waterways.

While walking around, we spotted an American Express office; they were offering affordable walking tours in many languages which included a ride in a gondola. Our experienced guide narrated a three hour excursion to our very small group, speaking to three linguistic sub groups. It was a perfect orientation to this most unusual city.

On our own, we went to Murano to check out the blown glass factories and showrooms. Just a short water-taxi ride away, the island of Murano is totally different from the tourist areas of Venice. Tours of the factories typically include a production line visit where you can witness the making of blown glass from start to finish. The last stop is the obligatory gift shop where temptation can be expensive.

'Did you ever think you'd be back in Venice?' I asked.

'This is such a romantic place; I wanted to come back here with someone special!' said Joshua.

'Is this mission accomplished?' I teased.

'I just wish I could hold you in my arms and not feel that we are embarrassing others. Maybe it's just me; maybe nobody around us would care or take notice. The world is evolving but when it comes to acceptance of same-sex relationships, I find progress to be excruciatingly slow. In 25 years from now, we'll have to come back; surely by then, the sight of two men holding each other or kissing will be commonplace,' said Joshua.

'Are you suggesting that this would be a nice place for our 25th anniversary?' I asked.

'Coming down the Grand Canal on a cruise ship to mark the occasion would be doing it in style, don't you think?' Joshua replied.

'Better start saving up now because 25 years will go by in a flash!' I concluded.

The Venetian sights and sounds never fail to impress; from the Palazzo Ducale, the Bridge of Sighs to the Basilica of Santa Maria Gloriosa dei Frari decorated with works of art by Bellini, Titian and Donatello, there is something for everyone in this distinctive and unusual city. We could spend weeks here and not have enough time to see everything.

It only took us two and a half hours from Padua to Florence but we spent almost as much time finding the Pallazo Vecchio Hotel: one-way streets and poor signage made the task difficult. Our room on the second floor looked like it belonged in a convent; stark, colorless and without a washroom. At a reduced rate, it was fine; the WC (water closet) at our disposal was an adventure. Calling it a water closet is certainly more appropriate than referring to it as a bathroom. Strategic planning of bathroom activities was a must; the small cubicle which is the whole washroom is also the shower. Therefore, the sink and toilet are in the shower. Best to refrain from using the shower until all other activities are completed; in this way, once you had finished your business at the sink or toilet, you're ready for your shower and guaranteed to splash water in every direction.

Our first stop on our self-directed walking tour was the gothic Cathedral of Santa Maria del Fiore, an 11th century structure covered with polychrome marble panels in various shades of green and pink. The cathedral's dome, which, at one time, was the largest in the world, remains the largest brick dome ever constructed and was the inspiration for Michelangelo's dome at St. Peter's in Rome. The Cathedral is on the Piazza del Duomo right across the Baptistery of St. John.

From there, we headed to the Vecchio Bridge, the only one in Florence not damaged in the Second Work War. All along the bridge are vendors, selling either gold or cheap souvenirs. Joshua and I had been warned of pickpockets so we took extra precautions. We noticed that thieves worked in groups; using cell phones, they would track potential victims and then swarm these people to offer help while robbing them at the same time. Their elaborate schemes work well as long as they are able to keep their operations under the radar.

No visit to Florence would be complete without touring the Uffizi Gallery, once the administrative offices of the Medici family. As the world's first public gallery, it contains some of the best art in the world by well-known artists such as Michelangelo, Boticelli, da Vinci, Raphael, Rubens, Rembrandt and Donatello. It was difficult to take it all in; after a while one gets saturated.

Around 6 am, we got into our car so that we could make a quick and easy exit from the city. I made a few turns to get onto a major thoroughfare and found it almost empty. It didn't take long before we realized that we were on a one-way eight-lane avenue driving in the wrong direction. I pulled the fastest u-turn I had ever done, one worthy of the Guinness Book of World Records. Joshua's face had gone white with fear. Ten minutes later, we were in the Tuscan countryside on our way to Pisa still reeling from our mistake.

43

In Praise of Clive

I continued my involvement with Lambda Ottawa upon returning from Toronto in December 1989. Now part of the Executive Committee, it was a good opportunity for me to make a contribution to a local gay organization whose membership was primarily professional gay men. Many of them were single and not into the bar scene; a Valentine Singles Party at the home of the President was a huge success. At this well-attended soirée, a handsome man I had noticed before seemed interested in me. Slightly older than I, Clive was tall, gregarious, and intelligent. So different was he from any of the guys I had relationships with previously that I did not think we would stand a chance of becoming a couple. Clive had been married; his two teenage sons lived with him. I was not about to move in with him nor had he asked me to do so. Ours was a relationship of convenience; we saw each other mostly on weekends. Clive was involved in musical publication; he wrote orchestration for many old pieces of unknown or lesser known Canadian composers regardless of the instrument for which it was originally created.

At that point, the world of publishing was not a mystery for me; I had written new material for young kids and was eager to get these to market. My newest collection of bilingual pre-school readers was gutsy; publishers are leery when the target market is not clearly defined. In time, I was able to convince the publisher that I had secured for my first collection, to take on my so-called 'Collection Parminou'. They agreed with the proviso that I find an illustrator agreeable to a royalties-only contract. Months of painstaking work by the artist yielded 56 exquisite cat drawings. In March 1990, the Collection was quietly launched at the Gatineau Book Fair. Clive, my biggest fan, was very proud of me. He understood the arduous process of getting a book to market.

The euphoria of my new books was countered by another death in the community. Mea had taken care of Leon not just to fulfill her promise to Norman, but because she cared deeply. He had been a pillar in our community; he would be sadly missed. Club Moustache would survive thanks to the strong foundations Leon had established. The weeks following his death were the saddest I had witnessed in a long while. Like vultures after prey, people showed up at the house wanting a share of the estate. Years later, people involved in this execrable asset grab were still not talking to each other. What is it that drives people to such low behavior? Norman and Leon would have been appalled.

A few months later, I suffered my first major bout of uveitis; I was away from work for two weeks. Stress at work and deaths in the gay community had left me feeling very low. Clive was a tower of strength; without his help and support, this major setback could have been much worse. He had a way of putting things in perspective; this was not life-threatening. Our discussion about whether it was worse to lose hearing or sight made me realize that it all depends on what's most important to you. As Clive was a music scholar, his hearing was more important than perfect vision. The opposite was true for me; my visual memory was my strongest suit. Not seeing the future clearly was partly to blame for my eye problems. I had read that the body is the messenger of the problems we try to conceal.

Clive was easily persuaded to come with me on my annual trek to Cape Cod. The *quid pro quo* was that we would include Halifax in our travels; he had lived there with his wife and was eager to go back. From Halifax, we crossed back into New Brunswick on our way to the US border. We wanted to spend time in St. Andrews By-the-Sea as neither of us had been there. This United Empire Loyalist town founded in 1783, is the home of the historic Algonquin Resort owned by Marriott Hotels. We indulged without a hint a guilt.

Unit no. 4 at Tillie's was ready when we arrived; kale soup was simmering on a back burner. Tillie and Clarence treated us like family. Her Canadian friends were important to her; in her opinion, we were considerate tenants. Any other Canadian referred to her by our small group was given priority. Never once did she have a bad experience with 'the guys from up North' as she affectionately called us.

From the moment we arrived, Clive felt right at home; it was as if he had been there many times before. Without the kids in tow, a relaxed Clive was the happiest person around. His broad smile confirmed that the environment was perfect for him. The informality of the town and of the motel we stayed in matched his low-key personality. On the Tuesday after Labor Day, when the town returns to a more normal pace, we settled into an easy routine; breakfast on the lanai, reading, lunch on the lanai, a jaunt to the beach, clean-up for tea dance, supper in a restaurant followed by a stroll along Commercial Street to see the beautiful people and to poke around in the shops. This leisurely lifestyle is wonderful for the first few days; as the week went on, we skipped the beach outing in favor of an excursion to one of the many pretty towns on Cape Cod where antique vendors and Arts & Crafts stores abound.

Escaping to a place far from Ottawa meant that I could temporarily forget the pain caused by the AIDS virus. For that reason alone, the respite afforded by the excitement and amusement I got in Provincetown fleetingly healed my wounds but less than two months after that trip, two more from my circle of gay friends had expired.

On the heels of that sadness, almost a year to the day after Clive and I had begun our relationship, we ended it by mutual consent following a long discussion at the Henri Berger Restaurant in Gatineau. We had been best of friends but neither one of us was in love with the other. It was a hopeless affair; there was no point in continuing.

I was beginning to think that I was not meant to have a long-term relationship. Of all the people I had been intimate with over the years, not one of them was the person I wanted to be with for the rest of my life. Settling for second best was not good enough for me; I was brought up with the notion that it was better to aim for the very best, even if it meant doing without for a long while. Although this applied to material things primarily, by extension, it could also apply to friends, partners or spouses.

44

From Trendy to Tawdry

Pisa was just as Joshua remembered. Completed in 1372, the Tower of Pisa, which is the bell tower of the Cathedral, was already leaning while in construction. Trusting souls willing to climb the spiral staircase to the belfry would need to wait until the doors were open to visitors. On that cold wet autumn morning, we chose not to wait; we took a few pictures of the tower, the cathedral and the baptistery. We bade farewell to Tuscany and set our course in the direction of the Alps.

The closer we got to Switzerland, the more dramatic the scenery became. Elevated highways, miles above huge crevices, gave us the impression of driving in thin air. Approaching the town of Aosta, the vistas were beyond belief; it looked surreal. I had noticed that Joshua had been unusually quiet for a long time. As I couldn't take my eyes off the road for fear of flying over the guard rail and down into the ravines, his silence bothered me. I had not noticed that his eyes were closed and that he was white as a ghost. There was no stopping the car anywhere to find out what was the matter. All of a sudden, I heard him mumble that he had a fear of heights.

'That's news to me,' I said.

'I know this is a very beautiful place but I'm shaking and my hands are sweaty,' said Joshua. 'I'll keep my eyes shut until you tell me that we have gone beyond this region. I can't imagine how they built these roads through such rugged terrain and on mile high concrete supports. Just the thought of it turns my stomach.'

'Well, well, I'm finding out things about you that I did not know,' I said. 'Guess I'll have to be the one going up ladders to change light bulbs or fix things on the roof.'

'Sorry, but there's nothing I can do about it,' said Joshua. 'Remember when we talked about driving from Miami to Key West? At the time I didn't want to tell you that I am also afraid of being on a long bridge over water. It must have something to do with a past life.'

'We'll just have to find ways to make it easier for you,' I said. 'For example, we can fly to Key West or better still, get there by cruise ship.'

What I had just learned about Joshua was not the kind of thing that would have scared me off or sent me in the opposite direction. I would need to be mindful of his phobias and he would do the same for me.

As we drove closer to the entrance of the Mont Blanc tunnel, the scenery was even more impressive; snow was falling even though it was early October. Opened in 1965, this 11.6 kilometer two-lane dual direction underground passage linking northern Italy to France is a major trans-Alpine truck route. I wondered if Joshua would have problems in the tunnel but to my surprise he was not fearful of it; however, the exhaust from the huge transportation vehicles caused us to choke a few times. It was slow going with bumper-to-bumper traffic. The weather had not made it easy for anyone trying to get to the tunnel; two hours after we drove out of it, it was closed due to poor weather conditions.

The Geneva Central Station was the ideal place to get help to find suitable accommodations. In a matter of minutes, we had booked a room at the Hotel Central overlooking the Confederation Centre. As soon as we got unpacked, Joshua was ready for a nap; I suspected that the stress of the elevated highways had been hard on him. While he slept, I went out to explore our immediate surroundings, and to find gay bars where information on the community would be readily available. A free organ recital in the Geneva Lutheran Church was just long enough for a short rest; back on the streets, I admired dozens of fountains each one very different from the other.

We were into our third week of travel; accumulated fatigue and museum overload were beginning to take hold. Joshua napped often; we did less visiting of tourist sites preferring to walk about. This way, we got a better feel for the city. Everywhere we went, there were lots of people strolling around: at the park overlooking the Water Fountain in the middle of Lake Geneva and in the 'Eau Vives' park. The city felt safe. Or did we think it was so because of the good things we had heard about Switzerland? So many green spaces, government and United Nation officials and friendly people everywhere. Geneva reminded us of Ottawa.

Heading in the direction of Lausanne, Bern and Zurich, we drove past the small town of Vevey home to the international headquarters for Nestlé where milk chocolate was invented more than 100 years ago. Nestled at the foot of the Swiss Alps, at one time the home of Charlie Chaplin, this idyllic municipality is right out of a fairy tale book. We regretted not having time to stop to see more than what we could observe from the car. The mountains behind the city literally drop into the lake at breathtaking angles. It was virtually impossible to take pictures that would do this place justice, yet any photos taken here would be picture perfect. Nothing is out of place, nothing is dirty and nothing is ugly. Utopia!

North of Zurich, we crossed into Germany driving on the east side of Lake Constance. Apple orchards as far as the eye can see; no wonder Apple Strudel is so popular here! We were heading for the Black Forest on our way towards Freiburg in the heart of a major wine-growing region, the primary tourist point of entry from the East. A university city, the old town is a mixture of Gothic and Bavarian architecture. There is no better time to visit than in the fall during grape harvesting; our timing was perfect to see this region in peak season. But again, we hadn't planned on stopping in this fair city so we moved on; final stop for the day was Strasbourg.

The further North we drove, the cooler it got. Strasbourg, the capital of the Alsace region is located right on the German border. In the core of the city is an island where we found a room for the night. This is where we experienced, for the first time, hotel hallway lights on motion detectors. After a walk around the tourist area, we went back to our hotel which appeared deserted. It was a bit spooky to walk dark hallways until the lights eventually came on triggered by our bodies in motion. We had come to expect that room keys had to be left in the slot near the room door in order to have electricity. We still laugh about the time when Joshua left the room and took his key while I was left in the shower in total darkness. He was gone before I could do anything about it.

Small tourist boats circled the Grand Island. It is a UNESCO world heritage site where a guide explains the history and geography of the island. Fascinating that the area alternated between the German and French ownership. The tour was a good overview of the city. This English-German, Catholic-Protestant town was a major commercial centre as far back as 932 and is still. Now the seat of the European Union, the city, once very polluted because the winds were blocked by the Vosges and Black Forest mountains, is a modern university town and serves as a transportation hub. According to the travel industry, it is the second most visited urban area in France.

The conversation that night at dinner was whether or not we wanted to go to England. Joshua was not eager to do more touring; he wanted to rest. I suggested that we should go to Bruges and if we liked it, we could spend our last week there. A friend of mine in Ottawa had been there and he liked it immensely. He had suggested spending at least 3-4 days. Satisfied that we would stay put in the same hotel for more than two nights, Joshua perked up a little.

Our plans were to leave Strasbourg early so that we would arrive in Bruges in daylight making it a bit easier to find a room. Other people had told us that this small city is like a miniature Amsterdam with canals and quaint buildings. It is also referred to as the 'Venice of the North'. That turned out to be an accurate description. We arrived in Bruges at mid-day; traffic was heavy and parking at a premium. A friend of Joshua had recommended a small hotel in the centre of town which would be easy to find in broad daylight.

45

Opening of New Doors

I felt ready for change when, in early 1991, I was offered a job equivalent to the one I had at Energy, Mines and Resources. The Public Service Commission was interested in me; they offered better career advancement opportunities with a work location within a ten minute walk from my apartment on O'Connor Street. After a nine year stint in the same organization, I felt the need to move to a very different department to get a whole new perspective on my chosen field of human resources management. My new supervisor agreed that I could take time off for a trip I had been planning with Clive. After only two weeks in the new position, I was on my way to San Francisco.

Our break-up meant that I would be alone on this California jaunt; that didn't faze me at all. I had dreamt about the 'city on the bay' for a long time; neither hell nor high water would keep me at home. Much of the original plans for the holiday were kept; I stayed at the Commodore Hotel as it was central and not overly expensive. The only down side was that I had to leave my rented vehicle in a parking garage a few hundred meters from the hotel.

I arrived just after a major earthquake that had done significant damage to the Oakland Bridge and City Hall. People thought it was foolish to go to San Francisco when more earthquakes were possible; the chances of a second terrible earthquake were slim in my opinion. Other than the damage to the bridge, which did not affect my stay, City Hall is where I saw the effects of the recent seismic event; scaffolding was everywhere. Large marble columns were braced with huge wood beams. It had truly been an earth shattering event; fortunately for me, it happened just days before my arrival.

From my base in San Francisco, I explored interesting places north of the city such as Sausalito, Petaluma, Santa

Rosa, Russian River and Bodega Bay. In the same day, my excursion had taken me from vineyards to the Pacific Ocean, from big city to quaint small towns, and from the hustle and bustle of Chinatown to the lazy flow of the Russian River. Touted as Sonoma's Gay Playground, I expected to see a lot of activity in and around the River; I was surprised that the whole area was deserted. It was off-season, I hadn't realized it.

South of the city, I drove in the direction of Monterey, Carmel and Big Sur. I had heard much about the incredible vistas on California State Route 1 near Big Sur (a winding road with 400 to 500 meter cliffs). For miles, the coastal highway parallels the ocean below. The whole area offers stunning views of the Santa Lucia Mountains as they rise abruptly from the Pacific Ocean. On more than one occasion, I was so distracted by the incredible scenery that I almost plunged the car down the embankment!

The work environment offered my only genuine escape; it was a cop-out and I knew it. Shortly after arriving at the Public Service Commission, I participated in a competitive selection process and declared the successful candidate for a middle management position — Head of Human Resources Planning and Employment Equity. This one-step promotion meant that I had people reporting to me: something I had always avoided. Managing a team required skills I didn't have; very little training was offered to help me get to the level of competence I needed. Slowly, I started having problems; at first, I was able to compensate and get by. At the end of the first six months, I knew it had been a huge mistake. It was time to move on, to go back to a stand-alone position.

In a year filled with short trips to visit family or attend conferences, I decided not to go to Provincetown. I had no real reason not to go other than wanting to break from tradition. Tillie had agreed to hold Unit 4 for me for the following year, thus hanging on to my seniority for my favorite studio. Going on the trip alone was doable but not what I preferred. It was much more enjoyable to share the driving with a trusted companion but they were in short supply at the moment Lurking at the back of my mind was the potential for a uveitis outbreak while out of the country. Unlikely as this was, it was nonetheless constantly in my sub-conscious, and my family doctor insisted that I carry a valid prescription in my wallet at all times.

Between bouts of uveitis and trips to Montreal to visit Geoffrey in the hospital, the months flew by; I was in a total daze. Hardly a day went by that I didn't drink four to five cups of coffee; the caffeine gave me a boost but it also played havoc with my arthritis. Quitting cold turkey brought on headaches like I had never suffered before. There was no turning back. My colleagues were urging me to do something to get myself back on track. The only solution I could see was to find a stand-alone job at the same level; I was in the right department as there were many level 4 jobs available which did not have supervisory duties. However, there was only one of these I really wanted (a Staffing Consultant position).

My social life had been transformed; house parties were a thing of the past. Going to bars had lost its allure; in terms of gay years, I was over the hill and of little interest to the new generation. A high percentage of people in my age group were partnered. I met new people at the Francophone Gay Men's Discussion Group meetings on Wednesday nights. Lambda events were also great for socializing. At the last meeting I attended, representatives from the Lambda Foundation had encouraged us to attend their annual fundraising event to be held at the National Archives Theatre on Wellington Street. We were promised an evening of readings from recent books published by gay authors. I had marked my calendar not to miss this October 30th event.

46

Bruges Revelation

At the Hans Memling Hotel so named after a famous Flemish painter, only one room was available for 5 nights. It was the nuptial suite! When informed of the rate, we stated that it was a bit more expensive than we had budgeted for, and the owner immediately adjusted the rate; we took it.

No room in any other hotel we had stayed in was as ornate as this one; furnished in French provincial throughout, the bedroom would have been perfect for Marie Antoinette. The canopied bed on a 4 inch platform was placed against the back wall on which hung three huge plastic angels; to one side, an armoire and at the foot of the bed in front of the windows was a seating area with two chairs, one two-seater, and a small serving table with a crystal chandelier overhead. Someone had carefully selected the fabric with a yellow and white small floral pattern that was used for the canopy, the bedspread, the room divider and the chairs. The carpet was pale blue, and the wallpaper in a blue and white floral motif completed the scene. In the large vestibule which opened up to the hallway and leading into the bedroom was another French provincial two-seater sofa in a bright red fabric. We sat in the chairs, looked at each other and laughed out loud. This room was gaudy beyond belief.

An enormous crystal chandelier hung over the grand piano in the lobby which we admired coming down the spiral staircase from the second level. Liberace would have felt at home. It appeared that the hotel foyer was used as a living room by our hosts. Informal as it was, we felt we were invading their privacy each time we passed through.

From the moment we met the owners, we knew they were gay. The noticeable age difference between the older gentleman and two young men left us wondering if this was a 'ménage à trois'. They drank cocktails and martinis in very fancy glasses;

these guys were not your typical gay men. In addition to the piano, the room included sofas, chairs, a fireplace, a television set and a live parrot in a cage on a stand. The room looked like an old movie set.

Adjacent to the lobby was the breakfast room in a flamboyant décor; there were three living room sets all in rose, 3 huge chandeliers and about 6 to 7 tables overlooking the garden. A giant gazebo had been modified to become a large birdcage. They could have filmed 'La Cage aux folles' here without spending money on props.

Bruges was a delightful place to walk around; everything was within a short distance from our hotel. As usual, we hit the historical sites first: the Basilica of the Holy Blood, City Hall, the Fish Market, the College of Europe, the Gruuthuse Museum and the Church of Our Lady. In this huge gothic house of worship dating back to the 13th century, we saw its most celebrated art treasure (a Madonna and Child created by Michelangelo circa 1504). This church is better known for its magnificent tower; it is the second tallest brickwork tower in the world.

Another tower of prominence is the Belfry of Bruges, a medieval bell tower added to the Market Square in 1240. For a small fee, access to the lookout point is via a narrow, steep staircase of 366 steps, the last part of which is spiral requiring visitors to hang on to a rope. This last piece of information was not given to us when we bought our tickets. Undaunted, Joshua and I followed the hundreds of visitors up the stairs to the first and second landing; the further up we went, the narrower the passage became. The third and final segment was not for the faint of heart or who fear heights. Joshua examined the spiral staircase and opted for staying on the landing as I climbed to the top. Although I'm not afraid of heights, I am a bit claustrophobic; at one point the passageway was not much wider than the average human body. With that many people climbing, turning back was not an option. I persevered and reached the top; the views of the city were stunning. Too bad Joshua would not see it. Just as I was walking to the opposite side of the landing, Joshua appeared, white as a ghost.

'Wow, you had the courage to attempt the climb,' I said.

'Curiosity got the best of me,' he said. 'Moreover, I wanted to be with you.'

'The views are wonderful from up here,' I said. 'I'm glad you had the nerve to come up. I'm impressed.' I added.

'I'm a bit shaky but I'm proud of myself for doing it,' said Joshua.

'It might be tricky going back down,' I said. 'I'll go first; follow behind me. If you get scared, stop and take a deep breath. You may want to hold on to me.'

'I think I'm ok with the descent but those steps are a bit narrow for my big feet,' he said. 'It would probably be easier if I went down backwards.'

'If that's what it takes to make you feel in control, by all means,' I said.

As we made our back down to the entrance of the Belfry, I kept thinking about Joshua and his desire to be with me even if meant facing a difficult situation. His fear of heights had not stopped him from making a huge effort to come and stand next to me at the top of the tower. It was a symbolic gesture, one that would prove to me that he would stand next to me even in difficult times, even when afraid. Through this incident, Joshua had shown belief in himself and trust in me. Whether he realized it or not, he knew that we would get through this together. He may not have attempted the final ascent without knowing there was somebody up there waiting for him. This experience was another manifestation of his willingness to be with me and was further proof that we would want to live together once we got back to Canada. One of the main reasons for taking this trip together had been to test each other; that had happened everyday in multiple ways. Ascending the tower was for me the metaphor that convinced me that he was the right person with whom I would want to share my life.

A boat tour of the canals of Bruges offered a glimpse of life in this ancient city from different angles not visible otherwise. It also brings people to parts of the city that are not seen by most tourists. One such place is a senior's home for retired lace makers. It was Emperor Charles V who decreed that lace-making should be a compulsory skill for girls in convents and *beguinages* throughout Flanders. At that time, lace was fashionable on collars and cuffs for both sexes. Bruges and all of Belgium for that matter is known for fine lace as well as exquisite chocolates.

Another Belgium tradition is beer-making. Joshua was in seventh heaven; in one very unique bar whose dimensions were 12 feet wide by 30 feet deep, over 300 beers were available. We sampled beer in several outlets; we ate out in excellent and affordable restaurants such as La Belle Époque, a French-Flemish brasserie reflecting a beautiful time in history with an Art Nouveau décor.

Our European trek was slowly coming to an end; during the final days in Bruges, the weather got nasty. We weren't expecting hail in October. It was a sign that it was time to go home. We drove all the way in the rain to Schiphol airport; heaven's tears were flowing down on us. We felt like crying as well but we needed to be alert for the long flight back. Holding back our emotions, we boarded our Martinair flight to Toronto (then Air Canada on to Ottawa) on October 26th. To our surprise, the majority of the people on that flight were Yugoslavians fleeing the war in their homeland. It made us appreciate how lucky we were to be living in a beautiful and safe country to which many would want to emigrate.

Sergio, Louisa's husband came to pick us up at the airport. They dropped me off at Connor Court, and he and Joshua drove to Gatineau to be reunited with his parents. Our 4,750 kilometer trip had been a great success; we were looking forward to the coming weeks when we would finally call Connor Court *our* home.

47

Life Goes On

My brother Geoffrey's health issues continued to be at the forefront of my mind. There had been talk of radiation treatments but the doctor in charge was away on holidays; he would have to wait for the doctor's return to know if they intended to go forward as planned. Any treatment was better than none; Geoffrey was anxious to start the therapy. In early October 1991, his prayers were answered; he was told that he'd get seven weeks of radiation administered four times a week in ten-minute doses. My father was visiting Phil at the time and together they went to see Geoffrey at the hospital in Montreal. Fearing that Phil would sugarcoat Geoffrey's health issues, I called my father and gave him a thorough briefing on the situation. I knew this would be most difficult for my father; however, I wanted to make sure that he was fully prepared for seeing Geoffrey in the state he was in: huge weight loss, red eyes and covered in sores that weren't healing very quickly.

Of the four therapies available (chemo, UVA, interferon and radiation), radiation had been selected as the most effective; he was told he'd have a 15 to 20% chance of prolonging his life by three to four years. Before starting radiation, he was on morphine every four hours. Right after treatment, he seemed to perk up; the pain was nonetheless obvious despite his best efforts at hiding it.

As if by magic, someone interesting popped into my life. Ken, a Scottish descendant and a true monarchist, had lived in Ottawa for most of his life. A public servant like so many in this city, he was well known for his interest in all things 'royal'. He worked in the Protocol Unit of the Secretary of State; he had been involved in many events related to the British Royal family. I met Ken at a dinner party in late September; I was surprised that he took notice of me. Charming as he was, my interest in him was tepid; I really didn't think that the timing was right as I was preoccupied with management issues at work. Furthermore, I had Geoffrey on my mind all the while. Ken would certainly notice that I wasn't ready to get seriously involved.

If nothing else, the diversion created by Ken was a relief I couldn't refuse. He was a well-mannered gentleman who knew what he wanted out of life. We dated for a few weeks before he left on a business trip; I wondered how he would feel upon his return. Would he still be interested in me when he got back to Ottawa?

All hell broke loose at work as one of my subordinates had a hissy fit in my supervisor's office. I was lectured by Joanna who felt that I hadn't managed Sylvia's performance issues to the extent she had hoped I would. My staff were not aware of what was happening in my private life; they had no idea of the stress I was under. One of my colleagues urged me to be more open with my employees and to explain to them the reasons behind my moods. This was no panacea but at least the staff cut me a bit of slack; I felt the pressure go down. This incident was a turning point for me; in the weeks that followed, I looked for another position at my level.

Never compare your interior with someone's exterior was a mantra that came in useful in the weeks and months that followed. I felt like a yo-yo; one minute up, the next, down. Claire called every couple of days with news about Geoffrey. The treatments were going well; he was hoping to get out of hospital by the end of October. His doctors were talking about a possible remission. Could this be really happening?

A play at the Théâtre de l'Ile caught my attention: 'Anne Frank's Diary'. Mary had suggested that we should go see it. With all of the difficult situations I was encountering at the time, I was afraid that I would find this story depressing. With a bit of persuasion from Mary, I relented; we went and were quite surprised with the quality of the performance. I had known about Anne Frank from the excerpts we read in school; my limited knowledge was significantly expanded that night. I vowed that if ever I got to Amsterdam, I would make it a point to see the house she lived in.

Stress had been part of my life for last 20 years; it made my arthritis flare up every once in a while. Though I hated taking the pills that were prescribed by my family doctor, the pain was wearing me down. I popped 'feldene' and 'novonaprox' hoping that I would be able to walk without a limp; it didn't work and moreover my intestines were a mess. At age 39, one does not expect to look like an old man, although in gay years, I was already a senior ready for the retirement home. I had given up on gay bars knowing that I would not meet my soulmate in any of those establishments.

The 'Wilde about Sappho' event sponsored by the Lambda foundation in November attracted a cross-section of the regional gay community. Most of the people in the auditorium were not the kind of people I'd see in the bars. This is what made these social evenings so interesting; there were interesting faces in the crowd that night. I noticed my friend Mark Lafontaine standing with two other guys, one of them I did not know. Not wanting to intrude, I stayed back and waved from a distance. Mark came forward to introduce the young man standing next to him; I assumed that he was Mark's partner. I greeted Joshua but paid no special attention to him as to not displease Mark. The three of them sat a few rows ahead of me. I couldn't help thinking how lucky Mark was to have found such a nice guy; they appeared quite happy together.

As far back as I can recall, I hated November as it was for me the dreariest month of the year. We remember the fallen on the 11th day, 11th hour. It seemed to me that, on average, more people died in November. Lester McAfee was the latest addition to a long list of fallen gay men in the Capital. I wanted the cycle of death to end; I wished for joy and hope. The purity of white snow in the last days of the month marked the start of a new winter season, a new cycle of optimism, and a chance to break away from a past that had brought its fair share of doom and despair. Christmas was just around the corner.

48

Moving In

Hearing about jet lag and having to deal with it are two very different things. Many times, Jean had told me how tired and out of it he felt after a long flight back to Canada. I really hadn't understood how the time difference affects one's circadian cycles. It took several days before my body had adjusted to the Eastern Time zone. I had gone back to work on the day after our arrival not knowing that I would feel jetlagged, and not able to concentrate on my work. A few days later, I left the office at midday because of an upset stomach, an intestinal flu was starting.

During our first weekend back, Joshua and I started getting the den ready for his arrival. We bought bookcases at IKEA which would house his collection of CDs, LPs and books on various artists. There was no need to have a definitive conversation about his moving-in with me. That had been decided before we left for Europe. If we had had tensions during our month-long adventure, we would certainly have discussed the impacts of these. We felt ready for commitment and consequently we worked on rearranging the apartment so that he would have enough space to bring most of his belongings to Ottawa.

Parcels addressed to Joshua sent from Amsterdam and Vienna arrived safely at 250 O'Connor. The information was logged into a register and each CD was assigned its unique numerical identifier. I marveled at how well Joshua was organized; his very methodical approach was a clear indication of someone who takes care of his belongings; if he did that with his things, he would likely handle my possessions in the same careful manner.

In the early days of November 1992, just under a year after we had met, Joshua had definitely left his parent's home and was now living with me at Connor Court. My fear was that he was not living in a place we had chosen together. He was essentially living in my surroundings graced with the art I had collected over the years. I promised that each little change that we would make to the apartment, we would make it together so that he could feel more at home. He certainly liked the apartment and was comfortable in it. It wasn't luxurious by any stretch of the imagination, nor was it a slum dwelling. All of it had been painted beige prior to my moving in; I saw no reason to change that at the time. After Joshua's arrival, we talked about putting color on the walls; this would be another way of making him feel that the apartment was equally his home.

'Do you believe in destiny?' enquired Joshua.

'I didn't before, but I do now,' I answered. 'Why do you ask?'

'I was thinking about us a few days ago and I came to the conclusion that if we had met say ten years ago, we would not have started a relationship,' said Joshua. 'I was not ready for a commitment at that time and I hadn't had a chance to sow my wild oats. At the age of 19, I wasn't looking for a long-term relationship. I had no desire to settle down with another guy.'

'What surprises me is that you are moving in with me directly from your parent's home without ever experiencing living on your own,' I said. 'Do you think you'll regret not having done so?'

'Living alone is not something I ever considered,' said Joshua. 'I would much prefer sharing my life with somebody, but not just anybody. From the first time I saw you, I was interested in you. It wasn't difficult to get references on you. It all started when I spotted you at an Ottawa Gay Men's Chorus concert at Centrepointe. A few weeks later, Mark introduced us at the National Archives during the intermission at the 'Wilde about Sappho' event but I don't think I registered with you.'

'Gosh, you were persistent,' I said. 'I'd forgotten about all of that. The first night we were together you had explained all you had done to get my attention.'

'Not only did destiny play an important role in our story, it is amusing to note the many commonalities that existed even before we met,' said Joshua.

'Ok, you've lost me here. What are you talking about?' I asked.

'At the top of the list is Gatineau,' replied Joshua. 'You were a teacher at the Gatineau Elementary School just down the street from where I lived with my parents. We were both raised in small towns where the Canadian International Paper (CIP) Company was the major employer. 'Company houses' built by the CIP on Poplar, Maple and Birch Streets are identical to those in Dalhousie where you were born.'

'You're right,' I said. 'We do have that in common. Anything else?'

'We both know Frankie Bouchez from Templeton,' Joshua added. 'One could call that coincidence or is it the *six degrees of separation*? We also have two friends in common: Mark and Henry.'

'I'll bet you a dollar that, over time, we'll find more connections and more commonalities,' I said.

I had definitely adjusted my sails to the prevailing winds. Finding a soulmate is like looking for a needle in a haystack. When you do, there is no mistaking it. A new phase of this adventure was about to start. Based on mutual respect and commitment to each other; I had every reason to believe that Lady Luck was on our side.

It could very well not have happened, as I learned from Joshua that on the evening of the Christmas party, had I not shown interest in him, he had decided that Don Goldberg was his second choice.

However difficult or long my search had been, it was time to turn the page. A whole new life was opening up to me with the promise, or a least an expectation, that things would be changing for the better, that wonderful experiences would unfold, that trips to far flung places would materialize and that our love for each other would grow with each passing day. A soulmate at last! A gay soulmate!